Heart's Desire Cottage

Prue Warren

VANTAGE PRESS
New York

This is a work of fiction. Any similarity between the names and characters in this book and any real persons, living or dead, is purely coincidental.

Illustrated by Tanya Stewart

FIRST EDITION

Published by Vantage Press, Inc.
419 Park Ave. South, New York, NY 10016

Manufactured in the United States of America
ISBN: 0-533-15240-2

Library of Congress Catalog Card No.: 2005904352

0 9 8 7 6 5 4 3 2 1

Contents

Heart's Desire Cottage

I
Wickham Lane

Janessa Gordon was nine years old, traveling alone on a jet airplane.

She knew when to fasten her seat belt and when to close the plastic table tray. She was more calm than the stewardess who offered her sodas and chewing gum. She was not scared and she was definitely not going to throw up.

Her Uncle MacKenzie Gordon stood inside the airplane terminal. Taller than anyone else, like her father, but with snowy white hair.

"Jessie, welcome to the city," said Uncle MacKenzie.

"Hi, Uncle Mac," Jessie grinned, shaking his hand. She liked him best of all her aunts and uncles because he never said embarrassing things like you're such a big girl now. Uncle MacKenzie loaded Jessie's suitcase into his little red automobile. It reminded her of a clown car in the circus, but it easily dodged larger cars through the city traffic.

Soon they turned down a narrow alley under a

green archway of trees. Jessie caught glimpses of old houses painted unusual colors.

"Here we are, Wickham Lane," Uncle MacKenzie said. He stopped the car under a giant maple tree. "And this is Heart's Desire Cottage." Jessie could scarcely see the house. It was covered with ivy and droopy bushes. But she thought there might be a tower with windows sticking out of the roof.

"I've forgotten my key," Uncle MacKenzie announced as he put her suitcase on the porch.

Jessie settled on the porch swing, wondering what would happen next. Her favorite uncle was absent-minded. It's a marvel he remembers where he lives, her mother would say.

But Uncle MacKenzie didn't seem worried. Instead, he stooped to the letter slot in the front door. He banged its brass cover three times. Then he bent closer to the slot and called into it.

"Wickham? Come here, Wickham. Bring me the extra key." He folded his arms and sat on the porch railing. They waited. In a few minutes Jessie saw a scrawny black cat trotting along the driveway. He had two white feet, one white blotch on his forehead and something in his mouth.

"Look at the cat," Jessie said, jumping from the swing. "He's caught a mouse."

"Good old Wickham," Uncle MacKenzie smiled. The cat hopped up the steps, then dropped his prey at Uncle Mac's feet. It wasn't a mouse at all, but a tiny leather pouch.

"Thank you, Wickham, clever fellow." Uncle MacKenzie untied the pouch and took out a key. He unlocked the front door.

Wickham stared at Jessie. *He knows I think he's an ugly old cat,* she said to herself. Wickham crooked his tail haughtily and led the way inside the house.

"First, we must give Wickham his reward," said Uncle MacKenzie. Jessie followed them through a long hallway to the kitchen. Uncle MacKenzie opened the refrigerator and brought out a tin of sardines.

The cat stood on its hind legs and snatched the little fish that Uncle Mac lowered to its paws. To Jessie, sardines looked disgusting. The moment she thought that, Wickham glared at her again. Then he carried his prize under the kitchen table and gobbled it up.

"He knows what I'm thinking," Jessie whispered.

"Always does," Uncle MacKenzie agreed. "He came strolling down the lane one day. He decided we needed help and adopted the cottage."

"Is that why he's called Wickham?"

"Yes, and he knows everything that happens on Wickham Lane." Jessie thought the cat nodded. She wasn't sure.

"But how did he bring the key?"

Uncle MacKenzie hung the leather pouch on a hook beside the kitchen sink. "When I signal—the letter slot—he jumps on the counter and gets the bag. Now follow me." Uncle Mac showed her a pantry room with shelves of food and dishes stacked to the ceiling. The pantry had another door to the driveway outside. In the bottom of that door was a small square that swung open when Uncle Mac pushed it with his shoe.

"This is Wickham's door. He can go out or come in as he pleases."

"He's very smart," Jessie said.

"He is indeed. But I lock myself out pretty regularly so he won't forget this trick. And he loves sardines."

When they returned to the kitchen, Uncle MacKenzie said, "I'm hungry too. The housekeeper has left us some fried chicken and fruit salad for supper."

Jessie found silverware and set the table. Wickham leaped onto the window sill and washed his face with one white paw.

"Uncle Mac, would he bring me the key if I were locked out?"

"I hope not," Uncle MacKenzie replied. "At least not until he knows you belong to Heart's Desire. Besides, I'll give you your own key."

Jessie felt relieved. She wasn't certain she could pick up a slimy sardine with her fingers.

II
The Big Picture

"Why is it called Heart's Desire Cottage?" Jessie asked at breakfast.

Mrs. Merryweather, the very round housekeeper, turned from the stove and smiled. "What's your favorite cereal, Miss Janessa?"

Jessie was annoyed when adults wouldn't answer a question, but she tried to not sound cross. "I like oatmeal with cinnamon and raisins." Her mother only cooked oatmeal on special days.

"Well, I just happened to make oatmeal this morning. Cinnamon is on the table and you can fetch raisins from the pantry. Third shelf on the left. Use the step-stool and be careful."

If Mrs. Merryweather won't answer my question, at least I'll have some special cereal, Jessie thought. She was finishing a second bowl when Uncle MacKenzie appeared in the doorway.

"Your niece wants to know how the house got its name."

"After breakfast we'll go on a tour," Uncle Mac promised.

"Mind you, stay out of the third floor. I'm cleaning up there this morning," Mrs. Merryweather cautioned.

"We will," Jessie said, carrying her bowl to the sink. "Thank you for the oatmeal."

"You're welcome, Miss. Three days a week I'm here and you may have oatmeal every time. If that's your heart's desire." She winked at Jessie and twirled her wooden spoon.

Jessie followed her uncle up a steep staircase behind the pantry. The stairs turned a corner and they were standing in room with sloping ceilings and a low window. "This was once a nursery for the youngest children," Uncle Mac explained.

Wickham the cat bounced from the window sill and ran past them down the stairs.

"Oh!" Jessie gasped. "He scared me."

Her uncle laughed. "Wickham watches the garden and listens to the birds. That's why he knows all the gossip of Wickham Lane."

They entered a wide hallway with many doors, all closed. Jessie was glad she wasn't alone. "This is a big place—for a cottage."

"It's called a cottage because it was built for the guests of Wickham Manor, the old mansion beyond the garden. Torn down years ago. What a spooky old castle it was."

They peeked into more rooms and down

passageways. If she had been alone, Jessie decided, she would be totally lost by now.

"Here's your room, Jessie. It was once the ladies' sitting room, where they took afternoon tea." Jessie had been so tired last night, she had scarcely noticed anything except the bed.

Uncle MacKenzie uncovered a little piano. "My Great-Aunt Carpathia played this spinet for her guests."

"I didn't bring my music," Jessie admitted. She'd promised her mother she would practice those awful scales.

"You'll find plenty of music inside the bench," Uncle MacKenzie smiled. "And the bookshelves are full of games. All sorts of amusements left here by the ladies long ago."

Jessie could hardly wait to explore her room, but Uncle Mac was guiding her down the main staircase. It was very grand, like in a movie, with curving banisters.

"Here's my office," he said, opening a door on one side of the cottage's front entrance. Jessie was surprised to see modern furniture and office machines. Colorful fish were swimming across a computer screen.

"Now you're on your own, Jessie. I should get back to work." Jessie wished she could stay and watch. "Across the hall is the parlor. That's where you'll find the answer to your question."

What question? Jessie wondered. But he was already pressing keys on his computer.

"Thanks, Uncle Mac. See you later." She shut the office door. Then, to be polite, she looked into the place he had called the parlor.

What a disappointment—more dusty old sofas and tables and drapes. But the fireplace was terrific, higher than her head and carved with a lion's face in the center. She would walk once around the parlor like a good guest.

Opposite the fireplace Jessie noticed a large gold frame on the wall. The title underneath read: HEART'S DESIRE.

Jessie couldn't imagine what was inside the frame. It was blank. No picture at all, like a turned-off television set.

She was about to leave when a fuzzy image started to form. Maybe a grassy field. A tree? Yes, an enormous tree.

Wait, there were children too. A boy leaned his face against the tree while other children ran away. Hide and seek, of course.

Jessie looked more closely. There were children everywhere in the picture! Children playing leapfrog and tag, kicking balls, jumping ropes, flying kites. Others were splashing in a lake and sailing boats. Some waved at Jessie as if she could join them.

So she pulled a chair in front of the painting

and sat down to discover what else was going on inside the golden frame.

On the left side a road appeared from behind a hill. Down the road marched five elephants swaying in a line. The last elephant was a baby hanging onto its mother's tail with its baby trunk. They led a parade of red circus wagons. Clowns carried balloons and whacked each other's bottoms. A beautiful girl in blue spangles stood on a prancing horse.

Now Jessie could hear music and a lion tamer cracking his whip. The lake had been transformed into a circus ring, ready for the show to begin.

First a family of acrobats somersaulted into the ring. A mother, father, two sons and a daughter. The boys, who looked rather like Jessie's own brothers, rode unicycles and jumped onto each other's shoulders. Their sister crossed a wire on her toes. She could toss her silver parasol into the air and catch it without falling. *I wish I were that brave,* Jessie sighed.

All the children were watching the circus. Clowns handed them balloons and pulled roses from their ears.

Whenever Jessie turned to a different part of the picture something new happened. Lions roared and snarled at the lion tamer. Poodle dogs sprang through hoops of fire. A man spun plates on sticks while he balanced a chair on his nose. Then horses with purple plumes danced and bowed.

Suddenly the band played a loud fanfare. The acrobat family reappeared on tiny platforms far above the ring.

The audience grew very quiet while the acrobats climbed onto their trapezes. They swung higher and higher. Then they somersaulted through the air, catching each other's wrists or ankles in the nick of time. Jessie was so excited she could hardly breathe. When they bounded safely to the ground everyone cheered.

At last, the elephants led a parade around the ring with all the performers waving goodbye to the children.

"Jessie, Miss Janessa," a tap on her arm startled Jessie. It was the housekeeper. "Lunchtime, your uncle's waiting in the kitchen."

"Already?" Jessie was dazed. *Hadn't they just eaten breakfast?*

"I see you've found Heart's Desire. Isn't it lovely? Reminds me of my grandfather's village in the mountains. There's the house and the barn with all the cows to be milked. And my pet pig, Oskar."

Jessie supposed Mrs. Merryweather needed glasses. There was no village or barn in this painting. Definitely no pig.

But when Jessie looked back at Heart's Desire there was no circus, either. The picture was fading. All that was left was the tree where the children had played hide and seek. And a balloon stuck in its branches.

Jessie ate a tuna fish sandwich while her Uncle MacKenzie finished his coffee.

"Uncle Mac, what is that painting about?"

"Heart's Desire? An amazing work of art." Uncle MacKenzie took off his glasses and rubbed his eyes. "That's the most beautiful beach in the world. With birds so rare, we assumed they were extinct. It's paradise."

"I saw a circus, with acrobats and horses." Jessie was puzzled. "Clowns? I thought I saw . . ."

"It's my grandfather's village," Mrs. Merryweather insisted. "When I was a little girl I stayed with him there."

"A circus? That's delightful, Jessie. I don't think anyone has mentioned a circus before."

"And kids playing games. Then they disappeared. What is it *really,* Uncle Mac?"

"Exactly what it says, Janessa. Heart's Desire. And your heart's desire isn't the same as mine."

"Or mine," chimed in the housekeeper.

"But it's a *picture,*" Jessie said stubbornly. *And maybe everyone in this house is nuts?* She kept that idea to herself.

Mrs. Merryweather laughed and tapped her forehead. "Some people don't see anything at all. They think it's a mirror."

"They see only themselves," Uncle MacKenzie nodded. "That must be boring."

III
Trip to the Store

"When your uncle MacKenzie goes shopping, he forgets half my list," Mrs. Merryweather said.

Jessie zipped the grocery list into her backpack. "I won't forget anything."

"Here's the money. There should be enough change for you to have an ice cream cone." Jessie tucked the money envelope into her jeans and strapped on the pack.

"Go the end of Wickham Lane and turn left. Not right, but left," Mrs. Merryweather instructed her for the third time. "Mr. Wong's store is five blocks from the corner. If you get lost—"

"I won't get lost. I hike with my dad all the time," Jessie said.

"But if you do, call for Wickham. He can guide you home in a flash."

"The cat?" Jessie would rather be crawling through a desert than ask that creepy animal for help.

"Wickham is very clever."

"He doesn't like me," Jessie said, glancing

around the pantry to make sure the cat wasn't listening.

"Wickham does act a bit hoity-toity. But if he really didn't like you, you would know it."

Jessie didn't care to hear what Wickham might do to people he didn't like. She said goodbye to the housekeeper and headed down the driveway.

At last—an adventure by herself!

Jessie had a secret plan: jog to Mr. Wong's store and jog home. Then she would have time to search for the garden before Mrs. Merryweather expected the groceries. Jessie had spied a patch of flowers and stone pathways, just a corner, from her bedroom window. There must be a way into that mysterious garden.

But first, her errand. Jessie set off at a quick pace along Wickham Lane. Ten minutes to the street. Eight more to cross the five city locks. Pretty good time, in spite of traffic lights, she complimented herself.

Mr. Wong's Grocery Store smelled spicy and was crammed with strange vegetables. Jessie took out the shopping list, but she didn't know where to start. She couldn't find many English words on the store's labels.

"Excuse me," Jessie asked a smiling gentleman behind the cash register. "I need some vanilla."

"Yes, Miss."

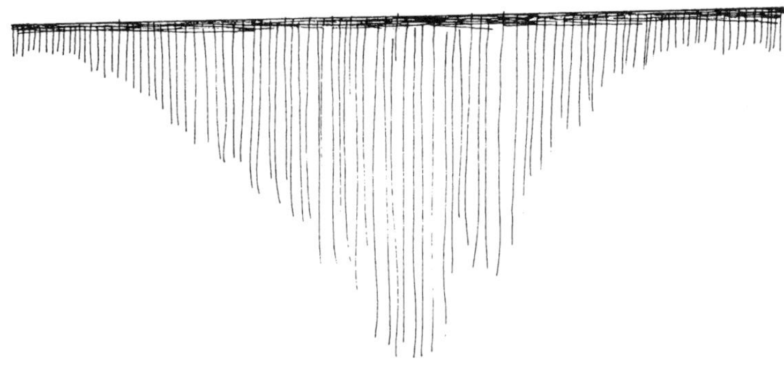

"Vanilla extract." Mrs. Merryweather was positive only *extract* would do.

"Oh no, Miss! I cannot sell you extract." the gentleman looked horrified.

"We're making cookies," Jessie explained.

"No, no, Miss. Too young. You cannot buy extract." Other customers were staring. The store was suddenly quiet. Jessie wished she could leave, but she had promised.

"It's for Mrs. Merryweather. At Heart's Desire Cottage? She sent me."

"Mrs. Merryweather? Oh yes, Miss. Sorry, Miss." He grinned broadly now and rang a bell on the counter. "My son, Tommy, will find everything you need, yes, for Mrs. Merryweather."

Immediately a handsome, but very thin, boy jumped down from a ladder and accepted her list. Soon he returned with brown sugar, candied orange peel, baking powder and the vanilla.

"Do you live at Heart's Desire?" he asked Jessie.

"Yes, it's my uncle's house. I'm spending the summer." Mr. Wong's son had black eyes and spiky black hair.

"I deliver their groceries sometimes and Professor Gordon lets me work on his computers. We're designing a new game."

Jessie didn't know much about her uncle's

computers. She couldn't think of a single thing to say to Tommy Wong.

After Jessie paid for her purchases and put them in her pack, Mr. Wong offered her a little box wrapped in scented paper. "Soap for Mrs. Merryweather. You take it please."

"I don't think I have enough money," Jessie hesitated.

"No money, soap is a gift. Gift for Mrs. Merryweather. Such a nice lady." Mr. Wong made a slight blow.

Jessie was blocks away before she remembered the ice cream. She didn't want it anyhow—ice cream cones were for little kids.

Daydreaming about the mysterious garden, Jessie almost missed the entrance of Wickham Lane. Things looked so different on foot, instead of zooming past in car.

The houses along Wickham Lane seemed even older than her uncle's cottage. What curious colors they had been painted: pink with green trim, or blue and chocolate. It would be fun to peek in the windows. But they were too high or covered with vines. Besides, she was in a hurry.

When the lane crossed a bridge, Jessie knew she was halfway to the cottage. She could take the next turn on the left, pass the front porch of Heart's Desire and go around the far side. The garden must be there.

GOOSE HOLLOW, the sign read, pointing left down a shaded alley. She would try it.

Soon Jessie found a pond with cattails and lily pads. But no geese.

She could bring Mrs. Merryweather a bouquet of cattails from the edge of the pond. But when Jessie stepped off the road, the ground turned squishy. Cold water oozed into her shoes. Jessie crawled up the bank, hoping her feet would dry before she got home.

Next she came to a crossroad. FOX GLEN, a sign read, with an arrow pointing to the right. That seemed the best direction. Blackberry bushes spilled over a rail fence beside the road. When Jessie reached for some berries, prickers stung her arm.

Fox Glen narrowed to a winding footpath. Dead end at a locked gate. Only a sway-back horse grazing on the other side. No fox in sight.

Jessie leaned on the gate and sucked the scratches on her arm. She would never find the garden if the roads didn't go anywhere. In fact, she wasn't sure she could find the cottage.

"I am not lost," she shouted at the crow on the fence rail. It flapped its heavy black wings and flew away.

The logical plan would be to retrace her steps until she reached Wickham Lane. Forget about the

garden for today. Mrs. Merryweather would be anxious for her groceries.

Jessie reversed her direction until she found the crossroad again. There was the sign that should say Goose Hollow. Now it read GOPHER HILL.

How could this be? Where was the pond? All Jessie saw were paths leading in four directions to empty fields. Even the sun was no help—it was covered with gray clouds. If only she had her dad's compass.

Something else was peculiar, but Jessie couldn't figure out what it might be.

Her shoulders were sore from carrying the pack. Her shoes were a mess. The scratches hurt. She was thirsty, too. Jessie rested on a rock by the confusing signpost. How quiet it was.

That was it—the peculiar thing!

Mr. Wong's Grocery Store was on a busy corner with cars honking and crowds waiting for traffic lights. It couldn't be that far away, but there was no sound of a city. Had the city vanished, too? All the people gone?

It wouldn't do any good to cry, but Jessie felt hot tears starting. She laid her cheek on her knees.

"Wickham," she said softly. Then louder, "Wickham, please help me. I'm really lost."

She was hunting in her pockets for a tissue when she knew something was watching her.

There he sat, on a fence post. She recognized

the white blotch on his head. "Wickham!" Jessie rose and strapped on her pack.

Lazily, the old cat arched his scrawny body and jumped to the ground. He chose the one path that Jessie thought couldn't possibly bring them home.

In a few minutes she saw the droopy bushes and the porch of Heart's Desire. Wickham slipped through his little door. Jessie used the regular door into the pantry.

"Here you are," said the housekeeper who was carrying a laundry basket from the clothesline.

"I'm sorry it took so long," Jessie apologized.

"We have plenty of time. I'll finish the laundry. Clothes before cookies."

"I could help you. I fold laundry for my mother."

"That would be lovely, Miss Jessie. But maybe you should wash your hands?"

"May I give Wickham a sardine first?"

"Hmph. You'll spoil that cat. What's he done today to deserve a sardine?"

Jessie told a white lie. "I thought he might be friendlier if I gave him a treat."

"Good idea. You can leave the groceries on the kitchen table," Mrs. Merryweather said on her way to the laundry room.

Jessie scowled at the sardines laid head to tail in slimy rows. She loosened one with a fork. *Ugh.*

Wickham was already waiting. His yellow eyes glowed.

As quickly as she could, Jessie picked up the fish and dropped it into the cat's raised paws.

"Thank you, Wickham," she whispered. "Please don't tell."

Jessie washed her hands. Then she washed them again. Wickham washed himself, too.

IV
Cousins

"Your Uncle MacKenzie is giving a lecture at the university this morning," Mrs. Merryweather announced. "He says stay in bed until you feel better."

Jessie's throat was scratchy and her nose was stuffy. A summer cold was the worst torture. Colds shouldn't be allowed during school vacation.

"What would you like for breakfast, Miss Janessa?" the housekeeper asked, much too cheerfully. Jessie groaned and slid under the covers. "Never mind, I won't even open the curtains."

Jessie rolled over and pretended to sleep.

"I'll be back later with some raspberry tea." Jessie heard Mrs. Merryweather's shoes thumping down the hall.

I'm not that sick, Jessie told herself. *A book might make me feel better. Exploring this room could make me feel practically cured.*

When she first arrived at Heart's Desire Cottage, Jessie thought her bedroom was ugly. Too much pink, faded flowers on the wallpaper and pink ruffled curtains. Later she noticed the walls were actually blue with silver stripes. The furniture looked more grown-up as well. Bookshelves, a real desk, and the spinet piano. Not bad.

Put some clothes on, Jessie said to herself. But when she opened the closet, her jeans weren't hanging on their hook.

"What happened to my suitcase? Where are my shorts and tee-shirts?"

The closest was full of weird stuff, skirts and old-fashioned dresses, like in the movies. "It's the cottage playing tricks on me again."

Jessie finally found some white cotton slacks. They had prissy lace around the bottom and barely reached her ankles. At least they were comfortable. The only thing she could figure out to wear on top was a dress. The puffy sleeves were tight and she couldn't fasten all the buttons up the back. But it was her favorite color, yellow.

Her reflection in the mirror gave Jessie the giggles. Wouldn't her brothers be shocked if they saw her, wearing a dress for once?

Now she was ready to try Great-Aunt Carpathia's spinet. She had promised to practice this summer, then sort of accidentally left her music at home. In the piano bench she found a songbook. The words were corny, but the tunes had easy chords. And she liked the tinkly sound of the little piano.

"I'm still pretty good," Jessie told herself after playing a lovey-dovey waltz with both hands. "Thank you, thank you," she nodded to the applause.

"That was so lovely," a voice answered.

Jessie whirled around. Two girls in frilly dresses sat on the window seat. They were smiling and clapping their hands. Their hair was curled in long ringlets that bounced whenever they moved.

The taller girl swished her dress toward the spinet and curtsied. "I am cousin Cristobal. Such a pleasure to meet you, Cousin Janessa." She pulled the younger girl forward. "This is my little sister, Wilhelmina." She poked Wilhelmina, who also curstied, but looked quite irritated.

"I want to be called Willie, and stop bossing me, Cristie!"

"You can call me Jessie," replied Jessie, without any curtsy. She had never met any cousins like these girls. They're harmless—just batty, she decided.

"We are so glad you arrived in time for the tea party," snotty Cristobal said. She pointed to a table set with doll-sized dishes, a teapot, and frosted cakes.

Willie circled Jessie. "How did you get here, anyway?"

"On an airplane, of course."

"On a hair pin?" Willie doubled over laughing.

"She means the train, you goose," Cristobal scolded. "It makes *hairpin* turns coming to the city. Carpathia says it is the most elegant way for ladies to travel nowadays."

"She's here too? Carpathia?" Jessie felt as if she'd taken a train ride backward in time.

Willie squealed. "Carthie's gone up to the Manor House with our parents. Oh Jessie, I think she's sweet on your brother!"

That will be news to my brother. Jessie smiled.

"My heavens, what curious footwear." Cristobal stared at Jessie's feet.

"They're running shoes. Tennis shoes? *MY SHOES!*" They did look odd with her outfit, Jessie realized. The cousins wore cute black slippers below their white pants.

"You're allowed to run?" Willie asked.

"Sure, sometimes I jog with my dad. I can do three miles. Well, almost." The two girls looked puzzled.

"Run like a boy?" Willie wondered.

"Of course. And I can beat half the boys in my class," Jessie boasted. "But not in this stupid underwear."

"Pantaloons," Cristobal corrected her. "It is not proper to run like a boy and show your pantaloons."

"Who cares?" Willie hopped about, showing her pantaloons.

"Wilhelmina, please do not encourage Cousin

Janessa." Cristobal pinched her sister. "After all, she is visiting from the Wild West. She doesn't understand how young ladies behave in polite company."

"Did you have to run from the Indians?" Willie's eyes grew wide. "I mean when they scalped you?"

Jessie stared at the cousins' long curls and began to laugh. "Gosh, no. We all have short haircuts—in the Wild West. We were not scalped. Listen, the only Indians I know are a baseball team and that's a different city. Wow, this is so confusing!"

"We shall have our tea now," Cristobal interrupted.

"Someday, Willie," Jessie said behind her sister's back, "I"ll teach you how to play baseball. If I ever find my regular clothes."

Cousin Cristobal poured raspberry tea and passed the cakes. "Excellent," Jessie said. She had never eaten frosted cakes for breakfast before.

"We'll play games now," Cristobal ordered.

In the bookshelves they found boxes of toys, marbles, cards and colored paper. The cousins knew all these old-fashioned games and taught Jessie the rules. Cristobal wasn't so stuck-up when she lost her cards. She yelled as loud as Willie.

Then they all danced holding hands, singing the silliest rhymes they knew. They ran in dizzy circles. They fell down and showed their pantaloons.

"Oh-oh, I spy your pantaloonies!" Jessie howled.

"You're the one who's loonies." Willie screeched. They laughed so hard their sides ached.

At last, thoroughly exhausted, they collapsed on the bed. Together they read a picture book about three girls and their adventures with a magic cat.

"Gosh, I fell asleep," Jessie mumbled, sitting up with a start.

She was talking to herself. Not a trace of the cousins. Even the teacups and games had vanished. Things certainly popped up and disappeared without warning at Heart's Desire Cottage.

With any luck—Jessie hoped, opening the closet. There were her jeans hanging on the door. She shoved the dress and white pants behind her suitcase. She felt so good in her own clothes again.

Skinny old Wickham was sitting just outside Jessie's bedroom. "Wickham, were you waiting for me?" She stopped to pet him, but he made a black streak for the stairs down to the kitchen.

"You look quite chipper," Mrs. Merryweather smiled. "How would you like some raspberry tea?"

"No thanks," Jessie said quickly. "But that soup smells great." Jessie brought a bowl of soup to the kitchen table. Then she sat down with the picture book she had been reading with the cousins.

"What a charming book," said Mrs. Merryweather, peeking over Jessie's shoulder. "Those girls wearing such fancy dresses with those lacy things."

"Pantaloons," Jessie nodded.

"My, my, they're having a tea party and playing games. It's a long time ago."

"I suppose so," Jessie said.

"Still, they look familiar somehow." The housekeeper set a plate of cheese and crackers on the table. "That cat could be Wickham, as a kitten. And that *is* a long time ago," she chuckled.

"Could be," Jessie said. Wickham twitched his crooked tail and headed for his cat door.

V
The Map

"I wouldn't know where to begin." Uncle MacKenzie ruffled his white hair until it was as spiky as Tommy Wong's black hair.

"You should have a garage sale," Jessie suggested.

"I've already called the Museum Thrift Shop. They'll send the donation truck tomorrow," Uncle Mac told her. "Tommy is helping me clean out this mess, before the Carriage House bursts."

"I'll help, too," Jessie offered.

"That would be wonderful, Jessie. Now where did that boy go?"

"There's some real neat stuff in here," Tommy called from deep inside the mess.

"Don't start that," Uncle MacKenzie warned. "Or we'll never get rid of anything. Come on, Jessie, let's load these cartons." They began dragging rubbish to the driveway and sorting it into piles.

"Where did all this stuff come from?" Jessie asked.

"The four winds, the seven seas, who knows,"

Uncle Mac sighed. "Whenever someone brought home the odd souvenir from a trip, we said Oh just stick that in the Carriage House."

Tommy stumbled outside carrying old wood skis and a plaque mounted with antlers. He was wearing a white pith helmet.

"I'm a famous explorer, returning from the deepest jungle!" He threw back his head and hollered like Tarzan.

Uncle Mac covered his ears. Wickham, who had been watching suspiciously, scrambled through his cat door.

"It must have been tough—skiing in the jungle," Jessie remarked.

"May I have these?" Tommy pleaded. "Please, Professor?"

"I could use this tennis racket," Jessie hinted.

Looking quite stern, Uncle MacKenzie held up his hands. "Stop right there! We must show some self-control. These are the rules. After we clear enough space so my car fits inside the Carriage House, we may then, and *only then,* each choose two items to keep. Reasonable items."

"Agreed," Tommy said.

"That's fair," Jessie nodded.

In another hour, Wickham Lane was nearly hidden by heaps of treasures and junk. "Phew, I'm beat," Tommy groaned.

"Me, too," Jessie and her uncle said together.

They all sat in the shade of the droopy bushes and gazed at their project.

While they rested Mrs. Merryweather brought them lemonade.

"My goodness, the Carriage House has finally exploded. I knew it would some day," she said. No one else laughed. "Say, if you're throwing away this hat with the lovely feathers—well, what is so funny?"

Jessie explained their agreement.

"Then I'll be back after lunch to claim my prizes," the housekeeper replied. "And I hope it is a BIG truck."

"Uncle Mac, was this really for carriages, with horses and everything?" Jessie squinted at the quaint building with its arched double doors.

"Absolutely. Before automobiles were common, Wickham Manor owned at least three carriages. There were stalls for the horses and grooms to tend the animals. A fine paddock where the vegetable garden is now."

"I wish I had a horse," Tommy said. "I'd feed it and ride it every day."

"Great-Aunt Carpathia had a snappy one-horse trap—that's an open two-wheeler buggy. I've been told she raced it along Wickham Lane and terrorized the neighborhood."

"That's such a weird name, Carpathia," Jessie commented.

"Didn't your father ever tell you the secret of our names?"

"What secret?" Jessie asked. "I never heard any secret."

"In our family," Uncle Mac smiled, "boys were named for rivers, girls were named for mountains."

"Wow!" Tommy said. Jessie was speechless.

"I'm a river in Canada. Quite rugged and handsome, that River MacKenzie," he joked, pretending to pose for a camera.

"Is your father a river too, Jessie?" Tommy asked.

"Jessie's father is the most famous river in the world."

"Niles? You mean . . . THE NILE?" Jessie gasped.

"Exactly. When Nile started school, the teachers thought he was a little boy who didn't know how to spell his own name. He decided it was easier to let people add the 's' and call him Niles. But his real name is Nile."

"Does my mother know about this?"

"I expect Nile mentioned it, at some point." Uncle MacKenzie ticked off his fingers. "Let's see, there was Uncle Orin. His river was the Orinoco in Venezuela. Then we have Cousin Dan, who is really the Danube. Cousin Ken, his name is Kenya."

"My brothers are Dan and Ken," Jessie said. "Boy, this news will rattle their cages!"

"What about the mountains?" Tommy asked.

"Well, Jessie's grandmother Anna is actually Annapurna, one of the highest mountains on this planet. And Anna's mother was Olympia."

"That's my middle name," Jessie told Tommy proudly.

"Don't forget the wild Carpathian Mountains. Very appropriate for such a dashing character as Aunt Carthie."

"Rivers and mountains," Tommy said. "No wonder we found all this gear for explorers."

"I'm pleased to report that most of us have traveled to our names," Uncle MacKenzie told them. "Even the ladies, in spite of those long skirts, trekked in their mountains."

"I'm definitely going to climb my mountain some day," Jessie declared.

"I know what I'll salvage from our sorting efforts." Uncle MacKenzie rummaged in a donation pile and pulled out a large paper tube. He unrolled a map of the world. "We can locate the entire family."

"We could post it on the bulletin board in your office," Tommy said.

"I have an idea!" Jessie jumped to her feet. "Let's pin flags to the map to show where all our names come from."

"Splendid!" Uncle Mac applauded. "Let's do it right now. We can finish this cleaning work later."

He had forgotten his stern rules, but no one reminded him.

Soon the map was spread out and tacked to the cork board above uncle MacKenzie's desk. Jessie offered to make the flags.

"All I need are toothpicks, some colored paper and glue. Or maybe we could use colored tape."

Uncle Mac hunted in his desk drawer. "Look, three colors of tape. Tommy, run and ask Mrs. Merryweather for toothpicks."

"Blue flags for the rivers, green for the mountains," Jessie decided. "Now we need pens to write our names on the tape. Scissors, too. Check in your desk, Uncle Mac."

Tommy returned waving a box of toothpicks. Mrs. Merryweather trotted behind, waving her spoon.

"What are you three up to?" she demanded. "I've never heard such a commotion. My goodness, that's an impressive map."

"Found it in the Carriage House," Uncle MacKenzie told her. "Jessie didn't know our family names are a geography lesson."

"Rivers for boys, mountains for girls," Tommy added. "Isn't that cool?"

"I'm making flags to show all our places," Jessie said, busy with tape and toothpicks.

"Putting our ancestors on the map," Uncle MacKenzie joked.

Mrs. Merryweather watched them punch flags into the world. "You know," she smiled shyly, "I could be on that map, too."

Three flag-makers turned and stared at their housekeeper. "Dear Mrs. Merryweather," Uncle MacKenzie patted her arm. "I've never asked your given name."

"River or mountain?" Tommy held up a blue and a green flag.

"Neither. In my family, children were named for cities."

"Red for cities," Jessie cried, twirling the last roll of tape on her finger. "Where should we pin your flag?"

"My grandfather came from Austria. He begged my parents to call me 'Vienna' for the most beautiful city in Europe. At school I was called 'Vi.' But my name really is Vienna."

"That's perfect," they all agreed. Tommy and Jessie made a Vienna flag. Mrs. Merryweather tapped her spot on the map.

"I was always a bit plump, even when I was a little girl. My grandfather made dolls for me and read me stories. He called me his darling Vienna Sausage." The housekeeper blushed as red as her flag. "Don't you dare tell anybody that, or there will never be another chocolate chip cookie in this house. Lunch in ten minutes."

"The Wong family should have a place on this

map, Thomas." Uncle MacKenzie touched China. "Let's find your parents' village."

Tommy looked embarrassed. "Pop used to talk about it, but I didn't pay attention. I just wanted him to be American."

"That's not satisfactory at all," Uncle MacKenzie frowned. "Ask your father to write down the name of his town. Tell him we will put a flag on our map."

"Yes, sir. Pop would appreciate that."

Jessie set the kitchen table for lunch. Uncle Mac served the salad and Tommy poured milk.

"What's for lunch?" Jessie asked. "We're starving."

Mrs. Merryweather put a steaming bowl on the table. "Well, I made a baked bean casserole with . . . with . . ."

They all looked at the bowl, then shouted at once, "Vienna sausages!"

VI
Flummery

Jessie pretended she was the queen in a long jeweled robe. One step at a time she glided slowly down the grand staircase of Heart's Desire Cottage. She held onto the carved banister with one hand and saluted her imaginary court with the other.

It was hard to not look at her feet. But if she tripped and anyone laughed, she could chop off his head.

WHOOSH! Something nearly chopped off her own head!

Whoosh! A flying monster circled the hall and dive-bombed Jessie.

"Help! Uncle Mac!" Jessie crept to the bottom of the stairs and banged her fist on her uncle's office door.

"Grup, grup," the black thing squawked, slapping against the walls.

"Uncle MacKenzie, it's attacking me." Jessie fell into her uncle's arms as he opened his door.

"What's all the fuss?" Uncle Mackenzie steadied her beside the umbrella stand. The monster settled on the chandelier, which began swinging and clinking like wind chimes.

"Grup, grup," it screeched, flapping its black feathers. Jessie could see the orange claws clinging to the crystals.

"Good grief, it's Flummery," Uncle Mac said, hitting his forehead. "I forgot all about you, poor old bird."

"Gimme grup, matey," the bird squawked.

"It can talk?" Jessie asked.

"Oh yes, indeed. Flummery is a fine specimen of mynah. Talks a blue streak when he's in the mood."

"What is he saying?" Jessie planned to move very carefully until she was certain the mynah wouldn't dive-bomb her again.

"He wants his breakfast. And lunch. I'm afraid Mrs. Merryweather will scold me for neglecting his food." Jessie had noticed that things didn't run so smoothly at Wickham Lane on the housekeeper's day off. "Come on, Jessie, we'll find Flummery some grub."

"CAP-TAIN Flummery," the bird fluttered. "*The Flaming Dragon* is my ship."

"He's rather vain," Uncle Mac confided when they were in the pantry. "His ship—the so-called *Flaming Dragon*—was probably an old trading barge. Flummery was some fisherman's pet."

"What does Flummery eat?" Jessie asked.

Uncle MacKenzie tossed her an apple and an orange.

"Insects, mostly, but he hunts those on his own. If you cut up the fruit, I'll find his seeds." Jessie arranged slices of fruit in a dish. Her uncle poured bird seed in the center.

"Quite appetizing, don't you agree? Let's sneak up the back stairs, Jessie. I'll show you Flummery's hideout." Uncle MacKenzie carried the dish.

"This was a guest bedroom," he said, passing through an archway.

"It's like my room," Jessie said.

"Except your room is at the front of the cottage. This room is at the rear. And the guests have a solarium."

"It's a sun porch," Jessie cried, opening the glass doors wide. What a delightful place: like a jungle in a glass box, with trees growing in pots and flowers shooting out of vines! In one corner stood a wicker bird cage and a shelf stuck on a tall pole.

"Should we close the window, Uncle Mac?"

"Leave the windows open. In the summer we let Flummery go outside and cruise around the vegetable garden. He never goes far. And he's useful, eating bugs." Uncle MacKenzie set the food on the tall shelf. "Jessie, can you whistle?"

"Sure," Jessie grinned. Her brothers had taught her to whistle between her teeth.

"Give us a blast."

Jessie whistled. Uncle Mac covered his ears. Then he called, "Captain Flummery, here's your grub." He nodded to Jessie. She whistled again, louder.

They heard whooshing in the upstairs hall. Uncle MacKenzie ducked as the hungry mynah dove to the shelf.

"Eat your grub, Flummery," Jessie said.

"CAP-TAIN Flummery," the bird insisted, ripping an apple slice with his sharp beak. "Captain Flummery of *The Flaming Dragon!*"

"Where did he come from, Uncle Mac?"

"India or Burma, I suspect." Uncle MacKenzie lifted a big atlas from a bookcase. "Of course, I found him in a pet shop." He opened the atlas.

"That's far away." Jessie studied a page with yellow splotches for land in a blue ocean. "If we knew where he was born, he could have a flag in our map downstairs."

"Jessie, if you fill the Captain's bowl with fresh water, maybe he'll entertain you with a sea story. I must return to my work."

"Now don't get excited, Flum—Captain Flummery," Jessie cooed, reaching for the water bowl. "Don't peck my hand." She filled the bowl in the guest bathroom and set it back on the shelf.

"Thank ye, fair maiden," the bird said, cocking his bright eye at the water.

Jessie carried the atlas to an egg-shaped

basket chair that hung from the ceiling. She crawled inside—which wasn't easy because the basket kept swinging.

"Gosh, you could get seasick in this chair," she giggled. When the chair and her stomach settled, she opened the book.

"Page forty-seven, page forty-seven," the bird cackled. He combed his feathers with his beak.

On page forty-seven, "Pacific Ocean" were the only words Jessie recognized. All across the blue water were scattered islands, some as big as dimes, some shaped like pickles. Some were only specks without labels.

"How did you get around the world to this cottage?" She wondered if he understood what she said.

"Captain Flummery's my name. Treasure's my game."

"What treasure?" Jessie demanded.

"Contra-band, matey! Pearls and gold, gold and pearls." The bird held a seed in his beak, gulped some water, and tilted back his head.

"Were they stolen?" *Now we're getting somewhere,* Jessie thought. "Did you steal them?"

"Secret," the mynah rasped, spreading his feathers like a black fan. "Flummery knows secrets. Treasure's my game."

"I won't tell," Jessie said, crossing her heart.

"The great Raja cries for his golden crown.

Buried in the sea. Great Raja cries for his pearly jewels. Lost in the coral reef. Lost!"

"Where?" Jessie pointed to the map. Flummery seemed to enjoy an audience, so she moved her finger on the page to encourage him. "I promise to bring your breakfast whenever Mrs. Merryweather isn't here. If you tell me about the pearly jewels."

"We set sail from Java on *The Flaming Dragon.* Bound east for Tanimbar and treasure." The bird's glittery eye followed Jessie's finger tracing the route. "Mind the charts, matey. There's reefs and jungles. Men that fly on palm leaves."

"I've found it," Jessie told him. "Tan-im-bar. It's not very large just a little island."

"Golden crowns they make on Tanimbar. They dive in the sea and bring up pearls. Black pearls too, rare as mermaid's toes. Gold and pearls is what we're after."

"You stole them? How?" Even if she didn't quite believe a talking bird, Jessie liked a good adventure story.

Flummery ruffled his wings. "Pirate secrets are sacred. Not for maiden's ears."

"Hope to die," Jessie coaxed, crossing her heart again.

"Night-time secrets."

"Please?" The mynah bobbed excitedly on his perch.

"We load coconuts at Tanimbar. But when the

moon is gone, late at night, our ship hides in the mangrove swamp. Captain Flummery stands watch on deck for evil spirits. Now the crew brings treasure from the Raja's palace. Gold and pearls. Stow 'em in the cargo, under coconuts. Now hoist the anchor, matey."

Jessie could imagine the boat slipping with its contraband through the dark swamp.

"We set sails for home. West to Java, calm seas ahead. The skipper says, 'Don't touch the treasure. It's taboo.' But sailors be curious rascals. They want to peek on their gold."

Flummery paused for a seed and a gulp of water.

"The very next night the sailors drink the skipper's brandy. They pretend to sleep. But Flummery sees. They crawl inside the hold and break the treasure baskets. They put on crowns and dance a wicked pirate jig." The bird demonstrated, hopping on his shelf.

"Wake up, Skipper," Flummery says. "The sailors make bad magic with the treasure! Skipper is angry. He shoots his pistol to scare the men. Too late, too late. Taboo is broken!"

"What's taboo mean?" Jessie shivered.

"Only Raja and his ancestors can wear the jewels. The sailors will be cursed."

"Raja's spirit flies on a palm leaf. Captain Flummery sees him in the clouds. He brings the storm, the Raja's curse. Monsoon and evil wind. Three days, three nights, *The Flaming Dragon* blows north. Skipper cannot steer the ship!"

"Then Flummery sees the land. Four degrees south, one-thirty east. Islands where the nutmegs grow. Watch out for reefs and coral sharp like daggers! Monsoon drives us to the reef. *The Flaming Dragon* breaks and sinks. To the bottom of the sea! All hands lost. The treasure lost."

"Then how did you escape?"

"Captain Flummery flies to a nutmeg tree." The bird strutted proudly. "Remember, four south, one-thirty east. Islands where the sharks eat pearls. Mermaids wearing golden crowns. Islands with the nutmeg trees . . . remember."

Thump! Jessie blinked and sat up in the swaying basket chair. The heavy atlas had fallen to the floor. Had she been dreaming?

"Flummery, where are you?" Jessie searched the solarium, but the mynah had disappeared. Was it a dream?

"That Flummery told me the wildest story, Uncle Mac," Jessie said when they were eating supper.

"Gold and pearls, pearls and gold?" Uncle MacKenzie laughed.

"How did you know?" At least it wasn't a crazy dream.

"It's the Captain's most famous tale. He only recites it when he likes someone."

"It sounded so real," Jessie sighed.

"Mrs. Merryweather lets him watch television in her sitting room. It's no surprise when Flummery spins one of his outrageous yarns."

"Could this story be true?"

"Interesting question." Uncle MacKenzie wiped his glasses and rubbed his eyes. "Although the facts are garbled, I'm inclined to allow some truth in the old bird's tale. For example, Tanimbar is a real place, famous for gold jewelry. And magnificent pearls are found in those waters."

"Flummery said remember four south, some other number—darn, now I forgot. And nutmeg trees."

"Yes, those numbers might locate a shipwreck in the Banda Sea. The Spice Islands are where nutmeg grows. I've always wanted to explore them."

"Then we could—somebody could—find the treasure!" Jessie jumped up, almost knocking over her milk.

"Dear me, are you catching gold fever too, Jessie? Don't forget the Raja's curse." Jessie sat down. She *had* imagined wearing a crown to play queen of the staircase.

"I admit," Uncle MacKenzie smiled, "Hunting for treasure in the South Seas is a fascinating idea.

But it's far away. And I presume divers have discovered any wreck by now."

"I guess so." Jessie tried to not sound disappointed.

"There's another consideration. Flummery is possibly the only living creature who could identify the exact spot on the right island. We'd have to take him with us. The governor of the islands could keep him in quarantine for six months."

"Quarantine? Like measles?"

"Birds do carry diseases. Poor old Flummery might be locked in a little cage for half a year. I doubt he'd survive."

"That's terrible," Jessie shook her head.

"Mrs. Merryweather would never forgive me. She loves that mynah. Even though she says he watches too many cartoons and is a hopeless liar."

VII
The Tower

"They don't want me around," Jessie complained. She was trying to draw a circus horse.

"Now, Miss Janessa, they don't mean to be rude. Your uncle is teaching Tommy a new computer program. They wouldn't notice if Heart's Desire Cottage blew down on their heads." Mrs. Merryweather pulled a hot tray from the oven.

"This horse looks stupid." Jessie scribbled on her sketch pad.

"Open the door to the hall. When they smell chocolate chip cookies, they'll be ready for a break." The housekeeper set a pitcher of milk on the kitchen table. "Once we pry them away from those machines, here's what you should do." She whispered her idea to Jessie.

"Do I smell cookies?" Uncle MacKenzie appeared at the door, pushing his glasses into his shaggy white hair. Tommy was close behind, admiring the tray hungrily.

"Sit down, gentlemen," the housekeeper motioned with her spatula. "Help yourselves."

“Thanks, Mrs. Merryweather,” Tommy said politely. “These taste much better than the cookies my pop sells in the store.”

“Thank *you,* Tommy,” Mrs. Merryweather smiled.

“Hey Tommy, you want to see the tower? Is that okay, Uncle Mac? I’m kind of scared to go up there by myself.” Jessie nearly choked on her cookie. She wasn’t scared at all but Mrs. Merryweather had told her to say that.

“Tower? Where?” Tommy looked interested.

“That sounds like fun,” Uncle MacKenzie said. “I should work on my book anyway, Thomas, so why don’t you explore our tower room with Jessie?”

“Wouldn’t catch me going up in that scary place.” The housekeeper winked at Jessie.

“It’s above the third floor,” Jessie said. “You have to climb a ladder. I haven’t tried it yet.”

“Sure, why not?” Tommy shrugged. “See you later, Professor Gordon.” Jessie put extra cookies in her shirt pocket.

First they climbed the main staircase. On the second floor Jessie unlatched a small door that looked as if it might hide a closet. “This goes to the third floor.”

“What a big house,” Tommy said.

“Much bigger than you think,” Jessie nodded, leading them up the narrow stairs. At the top she switched on a light.

They stood in a huge attic room crammed with trunks and furniture. "This is worse than the Carriage House," Tommy laughed.

"Never mind that. Look for a trap door in the ceiling."

"I found it." Tommy pointed to a square frame above the rafters. "Oh great. How do we get up there?"

"See that metal ring? Pull on it. Uncle Mac says a ladder will drop down."

"Sure thing, genius. I only have to be a hundred feet tall."

"Stand on a chair, genius," Jessie told him.

Tommy dragged an armchair under the trap door. "Hold it steady, Jess." By standing with one foot on each of the chair's arms he could grasp the ring. When he yanked it, the door panel tilted back, showing a ladder attached to its other side. Tommy shoved the chair aside as the wooden ladder slid toward them.

"Wow! This is neat," he said. "There must be windows in the tower. I can see daylight."

"Ladies first," Jessie announced, to show she wasn't afraid after all.

"First you have to be a lady," Tommy replied. "Be my guest, your highness."

Jessie hoisted herself onto the first step. The ladder wobbled, but she climbed until she reached the opening.

"Yiiick!" Jessie screamed and bounced backward, almost falling onto Tommy.

"What's the matter?"

"Spiders. Oh, *yick!*"

"You're a mess, Jess," Tommy snorted, brushing cobwebs from her hair and shoulders. "They're just itty-bitty dead bugs. They won't hurt you."

"I hate spiders," Jessie muttered.

"Okay, relax. I'll get rid of them." Tommy swished one hand around his head while he climbed the ladder. In a moment his shoes disappeared.

"Come on, Jess, this is really cool." His arm reached through the opening and pulled her up.

They were standing in the center of a six-sided tower. Each wall held a round window like a ship's porthole. From the six windows they could see treetops, roofs and parts of the city.

"What a view!" Jessie gasped.

Behind the trap door Tommy found a stool, a long tube and a three-legged stand. "Help me move these. I'm closing the trap so we don't fall through."

"This looks like a ship's spyglass," Jessie said.

Tommy inspected the tube and cleaned it with his shirt. "I think it's a telescope. We'll find out when I set it up." He screwed the tube onto the tripod and tightened the bolts.

"What does this say?" Jessie wiped a brass plate on the tripod. "Commander Arno—Arno

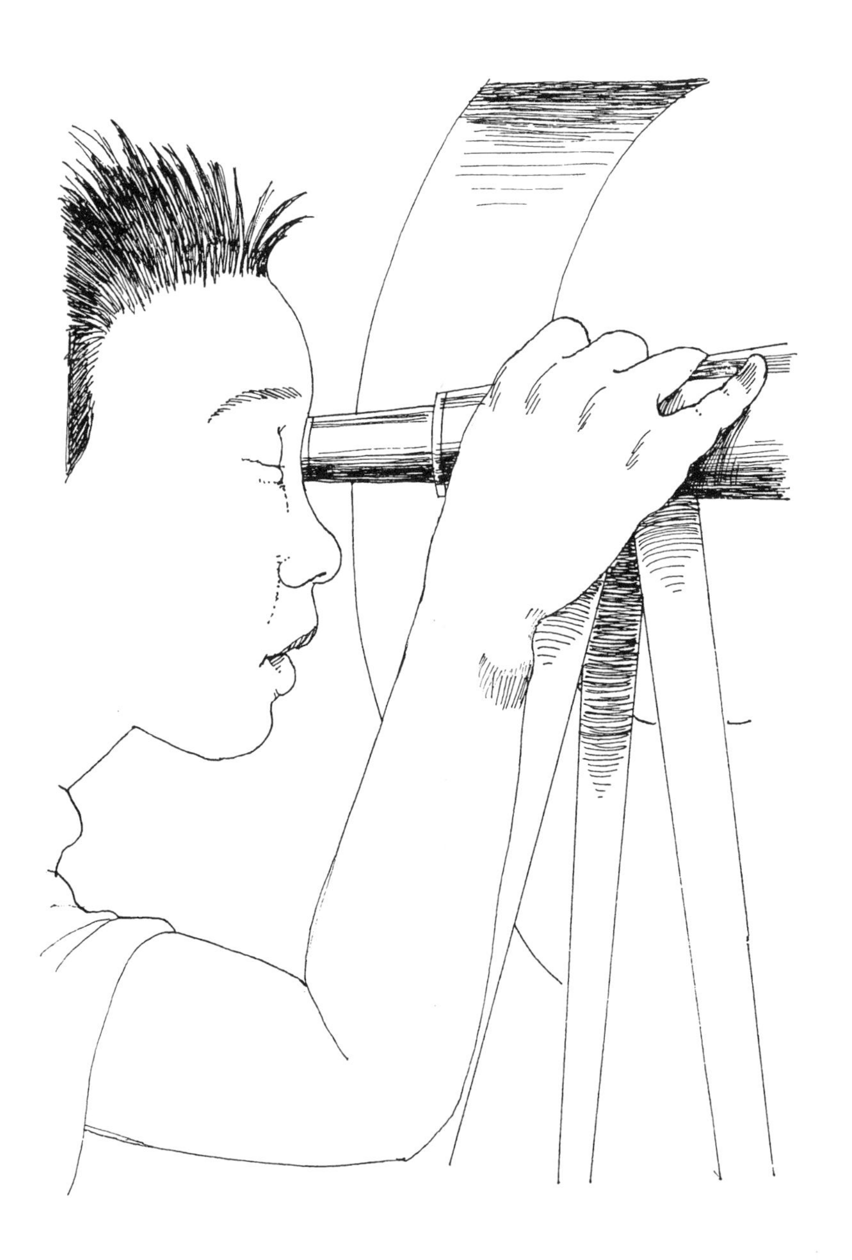

Wickham, Wickham Lane. What kind of name is 'Arno'?"

"River? Probably another river."

"I'll bet his teachers changed it to 'Arnold' because they thought he couldn't spell his own name," Jessie giggled.

Tommy ran his finger below the name. "Here's a date. July, 1905."

"A hundred years ago. Do you think this telescope still works?"

"Let me focus it." Tommy lifted the stand close to one of the windows. "See the Capitol? I'm trying to find it on the scope."

"I want to see too," Jessie said. "Gee, it looks so close, and the roof is really bright."

"That's why they call it The Golden Dome, Jessie."

"Let's see if we can find your father's store."

"Look for Bayshore Street. That's east, around this way." He moved the telescope two portholes to the right.

Jessie peered out the window. "There's Bayshore Park. We're getting close." Tommy trained the lens where Jessie's finger tapped the window. Suddenly, he stood back.

"Let me look," Jessie said, noticing the strange expression on his face.

"Wait. There's something." He bent over the eyepiece. "Really weird."

“I want to see,” Jessie begged. She stepped behind the scope. “Tommy, your father’s store—they’re tearing it down!”

“Nope.” Tommy carried the stool to the tripod and sat with his chin on his fist. “I saw the street sign.”

“Then it’s a trick,” Jessie said. “Maybe this isn’t really a telescope. It’s some kind of video player. We’re seeing an old video.”

“Shut up a minute, I’m trying to think.”

Jessie studied the location of Mr. Wong’s Grocery Store. Then she shifted the tube slightly to the right, then to the left. “Tommy, there’s something fishy going on.”

“Hmmm.” Tommy’s eyes were closed. He was thinking hard.

“There are people walking in the street.”

“Yeah,” Tommy mumbled.

“In the *middle* of the street. Because there aren’t any cars. Just a trolley and a couple of wagons.”

“So what?”

“Wagons being pulled by horses,” she explained. “Know what else is funny? All the people are wearing costumes. I mean like old-fashioned clothes. And hats.”

“That’s it!” Tommy bounded from the stool.

“Let me see the Capitol again.” He moved back two windows.

“Maybe we shouldn’t be playing with this thing,” Jessie whispered. “It’s spooky.”

“This proves it!” Tommy shouted. “You look, Jess. See those trees on the lawn?” Jessie nodded. “They’re real little. Okay, at school we took a field trip to tour the Capitol. The trees were tall, as tall as the second-floor windows. They grew. For a long time.”

"It's showing us stuff from long ago? Why?"

"Because it's old Commander Whatshisname's spyglass," Tommy explained, rubbing the brass plate. "When you look through it, everything you see will be the year—"

"1905!" they said together and slapped palms.

"Maybe that's the year he died," Jessie said. "It sort of stopped, like a clock."

"You're weird, Jess." Tommy returned to watching his father's corner. "If I told Pop I saw his store being built, he'd think I'm nuts and send for the doctor. Then my mom would cook up some nasty herb tea."

"Don't worry," Jessie said. "Your parents aren't even born yet."

"That's right," Tommy laughed. "They don't exist. And neither do we."

"That's kind of scary," Jessie said, but she couldn't stop laughing.

"At the top of our building—now, I mean—it says Erected 1906."

"Then the store won't be finished until next year—a hundred years ago."

"Jessie, you are one strange kid."

"I am not, I'm not even born yet, nutcase."

"Let's try an experiment." Tommy said, moving the telescope to another porthole. "We can find out all the things that didn't exist a hundred years ago.

Like the football stadium." He checked the eyepiece. "Wow! It's gone."

"My turn, my turn," Jessie hollered. "The freeway." She sighted directly at it. "Gone! Just a cornfield."

"My turn," Tommy said. "Here goes the Bayshore Mall." He snapped his fingers. "Poof!"

"That big skyscraper," Jessie tried. "Whoopee!" She looked again. "Too bad they tore down those houses. They were really nice." Reluctantly, she passed the telescope.

"My school," Tommy said. "Rats! Still there. But maybe I could make my violin teacher's apartment disappear—just kidding."

Jessie wanted to watch the harbor. "They're loading a boat with a round thing on its side."

"That's a paddle wheel," Tommy told her, grabbing the glass. "It's a steamship, *The Brazilian Queen.* All the way from South America. They're using a crane to load the cargo. A man fastens the hook to a crate and then rides up on the cable."

"You're hogging the telescope," Jessie protested, pushing him aside. "That's dangerous. What if the cable breaks?"

"He'll crash into the harbor and drown, goofball." Tommy paced around the tower, impatient for his turn.

"Now they're lifting a piano," Jessie announced. "Watch out, it's going to hit the smokestack. Whew!

They almost dropped that piano. Sorry, goofball, you missed it."

"Listen, Jess, here's the plan," Tommy said, pulling off his wristwatch. "We each get two minutes. You start counting when I say go. Then I'll count for you."

The system worked so well, they stopped fighting. Jessie explored the busy streets and people riding trolley cars. Tommy supervised the crew building a bridge over the river. They set up the tripod at each window and guessed which parts of the city they could turn back into farms and forests.

When they sat down to eat the cookies Jessie had brought, they noticed some dusty papers in a corner. "These are old charts of the harbor," Tommy said. "And here are plans for the city. Look, the Capitol."

"They even drew those little trees," Jessie showed him.

"I wish I could keep this and hang it in my room."

"We'd have to ask Uncle Mac," Jessie warned.

"No, it should stay in the tower," Tommy said. "Besides, if my parents saw it, I'd have some serious explaining to do. Uh-oh," he rose, putting on his wristwatch. "I was supposed to help my pop with the frozen food delivery."

Quickly they put away the charts and

telescope. After they climbed down the ladder, Tommy pushed it back into the trap door and closed the tower.

Downstairs, Uncle MacKenzie waved to them from his office. "Did you see some interesting views from the tower?"

"Yes, sir," Tommy answered, putting his finger to his lips and shaking his head at Jessie.

"We found Commander Wickham's telescope," Jessie said. She ignored Tommy punching her elbow. "We learned a lot of stuff about the city." Tommy groaned.

"Yes, yes," Uncle MacKenzie smiled. "I know what you mean. Very unusual instrument, that glass. I believe the Commander was a true visionary. He had dreams for the future of this city."

"I have to help my father now, Professor Gordon," Tommy said. "I'll see you next week. Thanks."

"Yes, certainly, Thomas," Uncle MacKenzie nodded.

When they were outside, Tommy punched Jessie's elbow again. "Never tell adults when you see crazy things, dopey," he scolded.

"Uncle Mac is different," Jessie insisted. "He knows what we saw. I wonder what he meant about dreams for the future."

"The old Wickham guy had those plans for buildings. He wanted the city to grow bigger."

"Actually," Jessie said, "I think when Commander Wickham looked into his telescope, he saw what the city is right now."

"You're kidding. Like when we looked in it and saw a hundred years ago—"

"He saw NOW," Jessie nodded. "Maybe even us."

"Jess, you are one strange kid," Tommy laughed. "See ya—next week."

VIII
Playing Mouse

Jessie spread her blanket under a row of giant sunflowers. This was her private spot behind Heart's Desire Cottage. She could see the back porch and her jeans hanging on the clothesline. And above, Captain Flummery's window where he flew out for bug hunts in the vegetable garden.

Could anyone see her? When she sat among the tall sunflowers, she felt nearly invisible.

Jessie opened the lunchbox Mrs. Merryweather had packed. Tuna fish sandwiches, lemonade, pickles, and cookies. Excellent—except for the whole wheat bread. Jessie peeled off the crusts. Mrs. Merryweather would never know.

"Hey, Wickham," Jessie called to the old black cat napping in the tomato patch. "Want some tuna fish sandwich?" Wickham blinked his eyes but didn't budge. *He's not fooled by bread crusts,* Jessie smiled. She hid them behind a flower, snacks for the ants.

After lunch Jessie unwrapped the painting

book and brush Uncle MacKenzie had brought her from the science museum.

"No paints needed," the cover said. "Brush with water, colors appear by magic."

Jessie flipped the pages. Horses, dogs, fish, cows, rather boring. It was a museum book, so of course it had to be educational. She would have preferred naughty animals like in television cartoons. Uncle Mac didn't watch television. He wouldn't know about those animals.

"I'll paint some pages anyway." She didn't want to hurt Uncle Mac's feelings.

"Darn it, no water," she realized. Now she was too comfortable to go back inside. She could spit on the paper—yick, that's disgusting.

"I've got it!" Jessie dropped the ice cubes left from her lemonade into her cup. As they melted she could wet the paint brush.

She was halfway through dabbing a page with ice water, when she noticed the colors were very peculiar. A green horse with a pink tail? It was strange that a science museum could mix up the colors this way. She painted a cloud that turned into a balloon with words coming out of the horse's mouth.

"I'm the horse of a different color," the balloon read. Jessie supposed this was a joke, like the ones Uncle MacKenzie made. What a goofy book.

After some orange sheep and roller-skating

cows, Jessie started on a mouse picture. As she brushed water on the paper, a family of mice appeared in their cozy burrow under a sunflower.

At first they seemed ordinary brown mice, with skinny tails and long whiskers. But when the page dried, Jessie saw clearly that the mice wore tiny human clothes with holes cut for their tails.

A fat mouse dressed in a plaid shirt and overalls sat on a chair made of bottle caps. He read a newspaper the size of a postage stamp. Must be the father.

Another large mouse wearing an apron stirred a thimble with a toothpick. That's Mom, cooking dinner. Baby mice hopped and scooted everywhere.

Two mouse children in shorts and tee-shirts were boxing and biting each other's tails. "You're in trouble if your dad catches you," Jessie said. She could almost hear them squeaking.

In fact, she really could hear teeny voices. Mouse voices. Not coming from the book but from a sunflower near her elbow.

Between the roots of the plant Jessie spied a burrow, just like in the picture, with a real mouse family scurrying around their nest. Dad reading his newspaper, Mom cooking. The children chasing their tails, chasing each other.

Jessie lay flat on her blanket to watch. What a noisy bunch. Her own mother would have a

HOME
SWEET
HOME

headache by now. Especially if her brothers zoomed up the walls and across the ceiling like mouse boys.

Suddenly Mrs. Mouse dropped her thimble. She rushed to Mr. Mouse and knocked over his bottle cap chair. They squealed at each other and waved their tails. *I'm glad my parents don't act this way,* Jessie thought. Mouse children huddled in a corner, silent for once.

Then the mother ran out of her house, dashing right over the painting book and her own picture. She was so excited, she didn't notice Jessie, who was trying to be invisible.

The father followed, and soon the children crept outside. They all sniffed the ground among the flowers.

They're looking for something, Jessie figured. You'll never find it like that, she wanted to tell them, running around in crazy circles.

One sunflower, the tallest, seemed to fascinate them. The parents raced around the stem. The children peered through blades of grass, their whiskers quivering.

Now Father Mouse reared back and took a running leap at the sunflower. As he climbed the stalk began to sway. He swayed too and dropped to the ground. Then it was the mother's turn. She wasn't as fat, so she climbed a bit higher. But the flower bent dizzily. She scrambled down, fast as she could.

Circus mice practicing their stunts, Jessie imagined. It was comical to watch them rush up the stem and somersault backwards. She hoped they wouldn't break their necks.

High on the yellow flower a brown speck moved. Then it squeaked the tiniest squeak. Jessie sat up and stared. It was a baby mouse.

"You naughty thing," Jessie said. "What are you doing up there?" The parents were exhausted from their acrobatics and the little mouse cried pitifully. "Just hold still, I'll try to rescue you."

Quietly, in slow motion, Jessie emptied scraps from her lunchbox and poured the melted ice from her cup. She didn't want to startle the baby and make it fall.

The rest of the family darted into their nest and watched Jessie. "Don't worry," she murmured, "I won't hurt your baby."

Jessie gradually sneaked behind the sunflower. Very slowly with her left hand she slid her lunchbox under the blossom. The mouse clung to the petals, trembling and sniffling. With her right hand Jessie slowly lifted the cup over his head. He looked up and his eye glittered like a black sequin.

Whomp! Jessie scooped the mouse into the lunchbox and slammed the lid.

Had she really captured him? She held the box to her ear. All she heard was the cup rolling around inside. She prayed he hadn't fallen out or been squashed by the lid.

Jessie set the lunchbox in front of the burrow and opened it. A tiny fuzzball shivered in the corner. "Go on, go home," she said. She tipped the box on its side, but he wouldn't move.

Jessie waited on her blanket. In a few minutes the mother poked her nose outside. She wiggled her whiskers and squeaked.

At last the baby mouse wobbled from the box and found its mother. Then the whole family sniffed and waved their tails, dancing around the little one.

They don't need my help any longer, Jessie decided. She repacked her lunchbox and folded the blanket. Maybe the mice would like those bread crusts for dinner. She gathered them to leave beside the burrow.

But when she looked back for their house, she couldn't find it. No sign of mice at all. She wasn't surprised. At Heart's Desire Cottage things popped up, then disappeared, quite often.

Jessie found her painting book flopped on its face. She dusted it off and a shiny object rolled to her feet.

Mother Mouse's mixing bowl, the thimble. Jessie could return it, if only the mouse family hadn't vanished. Perhaps they had hidden the thimble under her book. A gift for saving their baby.

In the kitchen Jessie found the housekeeper stirring her mixing bowl with a wooden spoon. For a second she looked like Mrs. Mouse in her apron.

"Mrs. Merryweather, see what I found in the garden?"

"My goodness," the housekeeper said, "doesn't that look like my old sewing thimble." Jessie handed it to her. "Where on earth?"

"Under a sunflower."

"I haven't seen this thimble since last summer. But you may have it, Jessie, since you found it."

"No thanks, it's too big for me." Jessie did not confess she'd rather eat worms than learn how to sew. In her opinion, sewing was only for prissy girls, like Cousin Cristobal.

It probably wouldn't be a good idea to mention the mice, either. Mrs. Merryweather might set traps in the pantry.

Jessie put away her lunchbox and took one last look at the painting book. The colors had faded. They didn't seem so strange anymore.

There was the mouse burrow, busy as usual. Now the mother was knitting instead of cooking. She sat on a cork beside a walnut shell cradle. Baby mouse was tucked in the cradle under a cotton ball quilt.

Safe at last, Jessie thought. But as she was about to close the book, the baby twitched his whiskers and blinked his bright sequin eye.

"Behave yourself, kid," Jessie smiled. *That mouse is going to be a problem child.*

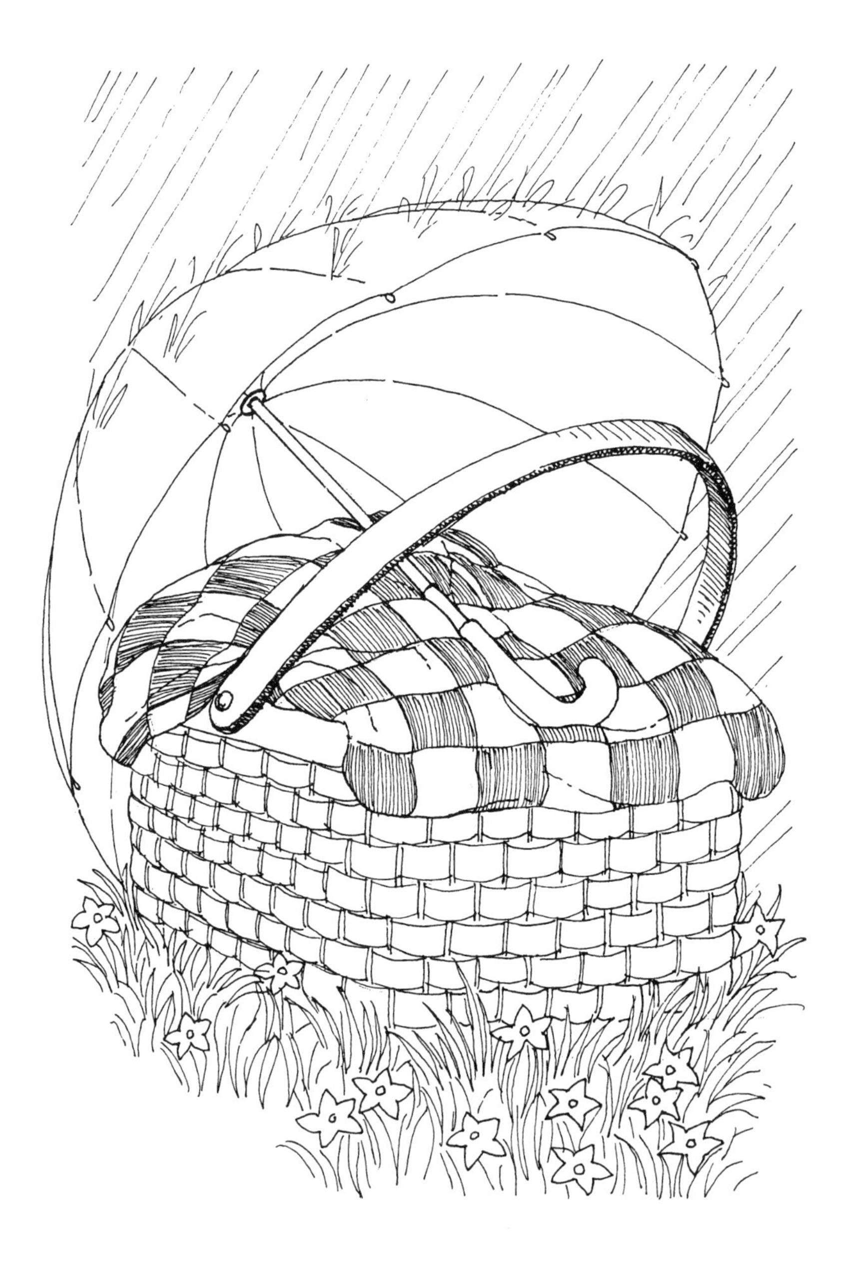

IX
Picnic

"When is it ever going to stop raining?"

"Tuesday, around noon," replied Uncle MacKenzie, consulting his watch.

"It's only Monday morning," Jessie sighed. She knew grownups hated whining, but she was cross and bored. Even Wickham the cat sulked on the window sill and refused to go outside.

"There's only one cure for these rainy day mopers," Mrs. Merryweather announced.

"Great idea!" Uncle MacKenzie's clapped his hands.

"What?" Jessie asked.

"A picnic, of course," said Mrs. Merryweather.

"Picnic? It's raining cats and dogs," Jessie protested. The housekeeper was already bustling about, opening cabinets, rattling the refrigerator shelves.

"I'll find the picnic basket," Uncle MacKenzie called from the pantry.

"Jessie, please bring the red and white

tablecloth. Also napkins, paper plates," Mrs. Merryweather ordered.

"It's raining," Jessie insisted. "We'll get soaked." *They must be deaf as well as nuts,* she thought.

In no time the basket was brimming with sandwiches, watermelon and peanut butter cookies. Outside Heart's Desire Cottage rain poured down harder than ever. Jessie found her yellow rain slicker in the hall closet. She picked out a sturdy umbrella from the stand.

"You're sure you'll need that umbrella," Uncle MacKenzie commented, pulling on a sweater.

"Where are we going, Uncle Mac?" Maybe they would drive into the country where it wasn't raining. How would they fit everything inside his tiny car? Especially Mrs. Merryweather, who was as round as the watermelon.

"We're going to the place we save for a rainy day," the housekeeper smiled. She took off her apron and put on a straw hat. Jessie was glad her yellow slicker had a hood. Mrs. Merryweather was going to get drenched.

Instead of heading for the Carriage House, Uncle MacKenzie led them to the box room behind the laundry. Jessie never went into the box room because it was filled with junk and smelled moldy.

Her uncle pushed aside a dusty trunk. There was a small door in the wall. He slid back the bolt and yanked the handle. The door creaked and scraped.

I'm not going in there, Jessie thought. *Probably full of spiders.*

"Pass me the picnic," Uncle MacKenzie said as he dropped on his knees to crawl through the doorway. Mrs. Merryweather handed him the basket, then squeezed through the opening.

They're leaving me alone in this big old house, Jessie realized.

"Hurry up, Jessie," Uncle Mac's voice echoed from the dark passageway.

"Take my hand," Mrs. Merryweather called. Jessie grabbed the housekeeper's plump hand and stumbled along behind.

Dim light appeared ahead of them. Soon they stood on a glass-covered porch. "The potting shed," Uncle MacKenzie explained. He waved at the muddy tools, pots and birdbaths. "I'm afraid I'm not much of a gardener."

They crossed the potting shed to another door. Then they were outside in a narrow alley.

Jessie stared at the brick wall in front of them. Twice as high as her uncle's head and stretching to the right and to the left as far as she could see. Weeds and vines grew up the wall.

"Where is that gate?" Uncle MacKenzie muttered. "Oh dear, I've forgotten."

Now what? Jessie wondered. At least it wasn't

raining so hard. In fact, the rain was only fog. She propped the umbrella against the shed.

"Professor, the lilac bushes," Mrs. Merryweather reminded him.

"Eureka!" Uncle MacKenzie pushed aside the lilac tangles and showed them a black iron gate in the brick wall.

"Is it locked?" Jessie asked.

"Not if you come on a bad day," Mrs. Merryweather chuckled.

When the gate swung open, Jessie saw trees and paths with marble benches. Could this be the mysterious garden she'd never been able to find?

Jessie tossed her rain slicker by the gate and stepped into a beautiful park. In the center there was a lake with families of ducks paddling in a line. While Uncle Mac and the housekeeper strolled along the main path, Jessie jogged around the lake.

"Sorry," she apologized to the startled ducks that scattered, quacking loudly. "I'll bring you some bread crusts after lunch."

"Phew, it's getting hot," Jessie panted, catching up with her uncle. Clouds floated past the sun. They sky was clearing, a bright summer day.

"Ideal for August," Uncle MacKenzie said, removing his sweater.

"Watch me do cartwheels, Uncle Mac." Jessie was showing off, and the first try was a flop. "That was just practice," she excused herself. By the third spin she managed a fair cartwheel, nothing to brag about. Mrs. Merryweather applauded anyway.

"Here's our favorite spot," the housekeeper said. She laid the tablecloth on a grassy mound, next to a statue of a chubby boy with wings but no clothes. "When you're ready for lunch, look for Cupid. He'll guide you here."

Mrs. Merryweather sat down on the cloth and knitted a stocking. Uncle MacKenzie opened his book.

"I'm going exploring," Jessie said.

It was a huge, rambling park, full of birds, squirrels and rabbits. There was a stream with speckled fish. You could cross the water on stepping stones like playing hopscotch or use the hump-back bridge. Jessie tried both ways.

She found bushes trimmed in shapes like ice cream cones and lollipops. Then flower beds with more statues. There were angels with wings and people with clothes, but no shoes. The fat stone babies playing in a water fountain didn't need any clothes.

What she didn't find was a single live person. Maybe everyone believed it was still raining. Jessie was glad. If nobody else was in the park, she could make as much noise as she wanted. She could jump on all the benches, shout, touch everything. And she did.

When she was hungry, Jessie climbed a tree to

search for Cupid. She saw his statue beyond the lake. Uncle MacKenzie was asleep with his book over his face. Mrs. Merryweather was unpacking the basket.

Then Jessie noticed something that made her leap from the tree and race to the picnic spot.

"Uncle Mac, Uncle Mac. Guess what I saw!" He sat up and blinked.

"Space aliens, a UFO?" he said wiping his glasses, which had fallen into the potato salad.

"No, but it's the same shape as a UFO."

"A giant paper plate?" asked Mrs. Merryweather, handing Jessie a normal paper plate.

"NO! A merry-go-round! On the other side of the lake."

"Merry-go-round? That's a new one on me—I've never noticed one in this park," Uncle Mac said.

"Let's ride on it after lunch. Can we, please?"

"We could carry our dessert over there," the housekeeper suggested. "It will taste as good on the other side of the water."

After they ate their sandwiches, Uncle MacKenzie boosted the picnic basket. "I could use the exercise." As they hiked around the lake, Jessie hoped she hadn't seen a mirage. When you lived at Heart's Desire, you couldn't be sure.

"Behold!" Uncle Mac shouted. "In the oak grove."

“It’s only a little merry-go round,” Jessie warned them. Four galloping horses with bulging eyes and golden hooves, one giraffe and a swan. All shaded by a pink and white striped awning.

“It’s lovely,” Mrs. Merryweather said. “Just like the carousel in our village at May Festival.” She sat on a log to rest.

“Where’s the man who runs it?” Jessie asked.

Uncle MacKenzie bent over a box tied to a post. “One token for a ride,” he read.

Jessie searched the oak grove for a ticket booth. All she found was a sign nailed to a tree:

PLEASE ~~DON’T~~ FEED THE SQUIRRELS

“There’s no place to buy tokens,” she complained. She sat down beside Mrs. Merryweather, very discouraged.

“Sshh,” the housekeeper replied. She was tossing bread crusts toward a squirrel. He nipped the crumbs, then thumped his tail and scooted to the tree with the sign.

Mrs. Merryweather poked Jessie. “Go see what he’s digging.”

The squirrel scratched among the roots like a little dog. Jessie tip-toed behind him. He swirled his tail again and scampered up the tree trunk.

Jessie knelt down and picked up a piece of metal, then another and another. Flat, round discs. She polished them on her jeans.

"Look what I found, Uncle Mac. That squirrel has buried treasure!"

"Do you suppose these might work for the merry-go-round?"

"Try it, try it!"

When he dropped a disc into the token slot, the machinery began to whir and hum. On the center pole toy drums and horns quivered, bells jingled.

Jessie jumped onto the platform. "Come on, Uncle Mac, it's going to start. I want the blue horse."

"The giraffe is just my style." They did sort of match.

"Quick, Mrs. Merryweather!" Jessie helped the housekeeper onto the platform.

"I prefer the swan," she decided. "Is my hat on straight?"

"All aboard!" Jessie shouted. The tin orchestra played a fanfare and the carousel lurched forward.

They spun faster and faster. Mrs. Merryweather held her hat and Uncle MacKenzie's white hair flew out like the horses' tails.

"That's enough for me," the housekeeper said when the music stopped. "I'm quite winded." Her hat was crooked, too.

"Me too," Uncle Mac agreed. "Here are the tokens, Jessie. You ride all you want. We'll be under the oak trees."

Jessie discovered she could command the

merry-go-round to go fast or slow. She could wish for happy music or a sad waltz. When she concentrated very hard, it turned in the opposite direction.

She rode all the horses and practiced tricks like a bare-back rider in the circus. The blue horse was the champion. He galloped the highest. When Jessie finished her last ride and kissed his forehead, she could swear he whinnied good-bye.

"I wish I could play in this park every single day." Jessie sat on the picnic cloth beside her uncle.

"But it doesn't rain every single day, Jessie."

"Uncle Mac, what is Mrs. Merryweather doing?" It seemed the housekeeper was laying a ring of peanut butter cookies around the squirrel's tree. "She's giving him our cookies," Jessie protested.

"Well, after all, we did ride on his merry-go-round."

"I'll have some watermelon," Jessie said, feeling rather ashamed of herself. Uncle MacKenzie sliced the melon.

"I saved us each a cookie," Mrs. Merryweather said when she returned. "My, that watermelon looks delicious."

They were all having a little snooze when Uncle MacKenzie's watch beeped. "Time to pack up and head home."

As they closed the iron gate, Jessie wondered if

she could find the park again. In case of rain. *Remember lilac bushes,* she told herself.

Jessie was helping Mrs. Merryweather put away the picnic leftovers when she heard a familiar sound. She pressed her forehead against the kitchen window.

"It's still raining here."

"Cats and dogs," the housekeeper agreed.

Uncle MacKenzie tapped his watch. "I know," Jessie nodded. "Until Tuesday, around noon. Anyway, it's a nice sound."

X

Wickham's Secret

"Wickham's trying to catch something under the front porch," Jessie informed Uncle MacKenzie and Tommy Wong. The office door was open. She could see they had finished their computer session.

"Oh, bother!" Uncle Mac pushed his glasses into his mop of white hair. "If that cat brings another dead critter into Mrs. Merryweather's pantry, she'll be furious."

"I'll get it out." Tommy jumped up, ready for an adventure.

"There's a flashlight in the pantry," Jessie said, starting down the hall.

"A broom would be helpful," Uncle Mac added. "You two can tackle the problem. I have work to finish."

Armed with the flashlight and the kitchen broom, Jessie and Tommy crept around the corner of Heart's Desire Cottage. They squeezed behind the bushes.

Wickham crouched on his scrawny haunches, guarding a gap under the porch railing.

"Can't see anything," Tommy reported, about to poke his head into the opening. Wickham shot under the porch, knocking the flashlight out of Tommy's hand. It rolled beneath the posts.

"Stupid cat!" Tommy yelled and squirmed through the hole on his belly.

"Don't go in there," Jessie said, but not loudly. "Could be icky spiders in the dark."

"WHOA!" Tommy's voice from below, then a bumping and a crash. "Help, Jess! I'm in a hole or something!"

"I'll get Uncle Mac," Jessie yelled back.

"No, no, pass the broom handle to me. You can pull me out."

I don't want to do this, Jessie said to herself, pushing the broom through the hole and wriggling after it. She felt the flashlight. She grabbed it and flicked the switch.

"Don't shine it in my eyes, dopey!" Tommy's head was level with her knees. He was standing at the bottom of wide stone steps.

"You okay?" Jessie asked, turning the light onto the stairwell.

"Scraped my elbow, that's all. Come on, there's a door. It must lead into the cellar." Tommy shook the dirt off his sweatshirt and then tied it around his waist.

"Maybe we shouldn't go in there."

"Well I'm going, with or without you, scaredy-cat."

"That does it," Jessie muttered as Tommy shoved the heavy door. "This is probably where Wickham is." She was trying to sound brave while she helped force the door ajar. But she checked for spider webs before she followed Tommy through the opening. It was damp and chilly and not very cheerful inside.

"Don't waste the batteries." Tommy took the flashlight. "Your eyes will get used to the dark. I can see some daylight."

Along the left-hand wall there were high, narrow windows. Soon Jessie could make out an enormous stone room below beams that held up the Cottage. "We're under the parlor, I think."

"Yep, here's the chimney." Tommy knocked the broom handle against bricks set into the wall. There was a hearth on the floor. "Somebody had a fire," He said, stirring the ashes.

"Could be ghosts," Jessie said, only half joking.

"Ghosts haunt attics, not basements," Tommy teased. "But here, whack 'em with the broom if you see 'em."

Jessie laughed in spite of being nervous. She carried the broom on her shoulder like a rifle, just in case.

"Nothing here. Let's try the other side." Tommy crossed a dim passage.

"We're under the main staircase." Jessie pointed with the broom. "It's spooky, looking at upside-down stairs."

"The computer room is there on the right," Tommy nodded.

"Then the kitchen, the pantry, the laundry," Jessie counted. More narrow windows on the outside walls let in daylight between the trunks of bushes. Nothing turned up beneath these rooms, except stacks of lumber and a few dusty boxes.

"We are striking out," Jessie said. "Where did Wickham go?"

"I haven't given up yet," Tommy replied. "You know, Jess, I don't think he was really hunting. I think he was leading us down those stairs."

"Why? He wants to show us something?"

"And it isn't a dumb mouse. What's behind the parlor?"

"Just a little room Mrs. Merryweather calls her sitting room. She watches TV with Captain Flummery. He loves the trashiest programs," Jessie grinned. "And he talks back to the cartoons."

"That bird's goofy, like this house."

"Then comes the box room—hey, that's IT!" Jessie hurried along the corridor with Tommy close behind, quite puzzled.

"What? What's it?"

"The *box room!* It has a secret passage to the

potting shed. Oh never mind, come on!" This was no time to explain about the rainy-day picnic.

But the cellar came to a dead end. It was very dark. Jessie took a deep breath and studied the last door. "This must be the place." She tried the knob. It wouldn't turn.

"How could Wickham get in here? This door is locked."

"Wickham goes anywhere he wants." Jessie smiled. "I'll bet he knows a secret entrance from outside."

Tommy stepped back. "Gee, maybe we should forget it. I mean, we're kind of like burglars."

"Ha, ha, who's scared now? I am going to find out what's behind this door," Jessie said stubbornly. "Give me the flashlight, there might be a key." She shone the beam around the door frame.

"There's no key," Tommy insisted. "Let's go. It's cold down here."

"Wait a sec." Jessie pulled her house key from her jeans. "Last chance."

She twisted the key in the lock until she felt a soft click. Slowly, slowly, they pushed the door open.

"Awesome," Jessie whispered.

"Wow, I don't believe this," Tommy gasped.

They stepped inside a warm, sunny room. Fancy rugs and plump cushions were spread on the floor. And everywhere they looked: cats.

All sizes and colors of cats. Cats and kittens playing, sleeping, washing themselves. The room buzzed with meows and purring.

Opposite the door, on a purple and gold cushion, sat Wickham gazing back at them.

"Wow, it's King Wickham." Tommy nudged Jessie.

"And his court." Jessie nodded. Wickham didn't look so old and crabby in his palace. The white blotch on his forehead glowed like a crown. "Pull up a pillow, Wickham says it's fine."

"Look at all their neat stuff," Tommy said, finding a space among the animals and their bowls of food. Jessie sat beside a sunken pool with a bubbling fountain. A tabby kitten jumped into her lap, ready to play.

"Where did all this come from?" Tommy wondered. "Who feeds them? Cats don't open cans of tuna fish by themselves."

"What difference does it make?" Jessie dangled a yarn mouse for the kitten.

"Well, cat's don't shop at the Bayshore Mall for rugs and pillows."

"Oh, be quiet!" Jessie threw the toy mouse at Tommy's head. "We're guests and it's not polite to point at people's—I mean cats'—furniture."

"Okay, okay, but look at this tree house thing." Tommy tapped a thick post that rose from the floor and grew into the rafters. Branches stuck out in all directions with cats perched on them. Tommy had climbed halfway up the trunk when a big orange cat opened one eye and leaped onto his shoulder.

"Ouch!" Tommy dropped to the floor, with the creature standing on his chest.

"Serves you right," Jessie laughed.

"Get him off me. I don't even like cats!" Tommy scowled into the wide orange face. The cat licked the boy's ears. "Yikes, it's slobbering on me!"

Jessie laughed and laughed, rolling on the carpet with a dozen frisky kittens who tickled her knees and nibbled her fingers.

"Hey, Jess, do you think these cats belong to anybody?" Tommy sat up, wiping his ears. "Maybe they're all the lost cats in the city."

"Some of them have collars. They don't look lost."

"What are they doing here? There must be a hundred of them."

"Maybe this is like their clubhouse." Jessie started laughing again, so hard she sputtered. "We think they're outside hunting mice, working all day. When they're really down here, hanging out in the Wickham Lane Clubhouse."

"Jess, you're as nutty as this dumb cat. Quit following me," Tommy said, pushing the orange cat with his foot.

"He likes you. And he doesn't have a collar. Take him home, Thomas."

"Mom would kill me."

"Tell her he'll catch mice in the store." Jessie glanced at Wickham, who seemed to approve.

"She will absolutely kill me." The cat rubbed his ankles. "I could hide him in the delivery shed. Pretend he just showed up there."

"How are you going to get him home?"

Tommy hesitated, while the orange cat waited patiently between his feet. "All right," he sighed. "You win." He made a sling with his sweatshirt and lifted the cat inside. It curled into a fat furry ball and purred. "This is going to be nothing but trouble," Tommy grumbled.

"That's his name—TROUBLE," Jessie said. She picked up the flashlight and the broom.

"Hurry Jess, he's heavy." Tommy started for the door with the cat bundle draped over his shoulder.

"Bye-bye, kitties," Jessie called. "Thanks, Wickham. See you later." The lock clicked behind them.

"Jess, we can't crawl under the porch with this animal."

"I've seen a wooden door leaning against the house. Near the laundry room. It must be another way out of this basement."

Across the passageway they found stone steps rising upward into darkness. "It's closed off," Tommy said. "We're blocked."

Jessie shone the flashlight on the slanting barricade. "Look for a handle or something."

"I see it!" Tommy showed her latch that fastened two planks together in the middle. "Piece of cake—we only need to open one side to get out."

While Jessie held the light and guarded the cat's sling, Tommy pried the latch. Then he pushed back the plank.

Sunlight almost blinded them as they climbed onto the lawn. "Nobody saw us," Jessie blinked. "Quick, close it and don't let it slam."

"Are you going to tell your uncle what we found?"

"Not me." Jessie crossed her heart. *He probably knows anyhow,* she said to herself. He probably even . . . who could guess?

"Me neither. I've got enough *trouble* explaining this cat. Help me think of a good story."

"Tell your parents the truth. The cat jumped out of a tree and knocked you down," Jessie teased.

"Thanks a heap, kid." He hoisted the sling. "Okay, big guy, we're out of here."

At that moment Mr. Wong's delivery van rumbled up the driveway. "Oh, rats," Tommy frowned. "Here's Pop with Mrs. Merryweather's order."

Jessie took charge. "You help unload the groceries. While your father's inside, I'll hide the cat in the van. I sure hope he doesn't get car sick."

"There should be empty boxes in the rear. Stick him in a box next to the spare tire, so I can find him fast."

"Got it." Jessie waved to Mr. Wong.

"And close the top," Tommy whispered. "So he can't escape."

"He's sound asleep," Jessie said. "Don't worry, he won't make trouble. Not yet, anyway."

XI
Birthday Party

"Tomorrow is your last day at Heart's Desire Cottage," Mrs. Merryweather sighed. "Summer is rushing by so fast."

"Don't remind me," Jessie muttered. "I'm packed, but I'm not ready." *Not ready for school either,* she thought.

"Then we must have The Birthday Party to cheer us up!" Uncle MacKenzie clapped his hands so loudly that Captain Flummery *whooshed* down the grand staircase and landed on the chandelier. Prisms fluttered and tinkled. Then he *whooshed* down the hall and plopped onto the kitchen floor.

"Of course you're invited, Flummery," Uncle Mac said.

"You are *not* invited into the kitchen, however," the housekeeper scolded. "Now shoo, Flummery, go watch television."

"Cap-tain Flummery," the mynah insisted, flopping off to the sitting room.

"We'll invite Wickham, certainly. And Tommy, with his terrifying orange cat." Uncle MacKenzie was fairly skipping to his office. "I'll send a message to Wong's Store right now."

"Chocolate cake with coconut frosting? Or apple spice cake with lemon icing?" Mrs. Merryweather tapped her spoon against her recipe shelf.

"It's not my birthday," Jessie said, "But I vote for chocolate." She felt better, now that the housekeeper was smiling again.

"It's nobody's birthday," Mrs. Merryweather explained patiently. "No reason to wait for your birthday, Jessie. You won't be here. I've stopped counting my birthdays, and your uncle doesn't remember his. We would never have a party at that rate." *Like a rainy-day picnic,* Jessie supposed.

"We declare Aunt Carpathia's birthday whenever a party is necessary," Uncle Mac added, returning from his computer.

"Shouldn't we invite Carpathia, too?" Jessie knew she sounded sassy, but she couldn't help herself when wacky things started to happen on Wickham Lane.

"Perhaps she'll turn up." Uncle MacKenzie stopped very still and smiled toward a place Jessie couldn't see. "But she travels a great deal now . . . remarkable for someone her age."

"Jessie, you can help me plan the menu," Mrs. Merryweather interrupted. "Shall we synchronize our watches, Professor Gordon?" She didn't own a watch, so she pointed her spoon at the kitchen clock.

"Tomorrow at fourteen hours. Two o'clock on the dot, that's the party hour," Uncle MacKenzie announced, quite himself again.

"That's when my father is coming to pick me up," Jessie reminded them.

"Perfect," Uncle Mac grinned. "After all, Carthie was his Great-Aunt, too. Isn't it lucky Nile had business in the city so he could join us?"

"Plenty of time before your airplane leaves," the housekeeper added. "Scoot aside, Wickham, we have work to do." The old cat twitched his crooked tail and headed for his little door.

The next morning Jessie's suitcase lay on the window seat. Her coat still hung in the closet. Now the bedroom seemed small and dingy again, like the day she had arrived at Heart's Desire Cottage. Aunt Carpathia's spinet was closed. The tea table was bare.

"This room *wants* me to go home," she said aloud. She shoved her suitcase into the dark hallway. "This house is dusty and moldy. And everyone here acts like a nutcase."

Immediately Jessie felt ashamed. In her whole life she had never had so many adventures by herself. Secrets her parents could never guess, secrets Uncle MacKenzie and Mrs. Merryweather wouldn't tell. So stop being a crab, she told herself.

"Can I help?" Jessie asked the housekeeper in the kitchen. "I've washed my hands."

"Certainly, Miss Janessa. Even though it's my day off, I wouldn't miss a Carpathia birthday party for the world. First, eat your breakfast."

Oatmeal with raisins and cinnamon, the best. "Thank you," Jessie said.

After breakfast Mrs. Merryweather sent Jessie to the box room. "Find the birthday decorations," the housekeeper ordered. "And anything festive."

Jessie hoped spiders hadn't invaded the creepy box room. She was startled to see Wickham sitting on a box marked MISC, whatever that meant. "Listen Wickham, where are the birthday party decorations?" If you're so smart, she added to herself.

Wickham crooked his tail and jumped to another carton. He stretched haughtily, then disappeared. "Thanks, old buddy. He still doesn't like me, I bet."

Jessie opened a dozen cartons of dishes and total junk before she reached Wickham's choice. "Wherever you are, Cat, this had better be the one."

It was! Garlands and party hats exploded onto her feet. Jessie wrestled the box to the parlor, where Mrs. Merryweather was fussing over the party table.

"You're in charge of decorating, Jessie. There's a ladder in the laundry. And could you create a centerpiece for this table? Lovely. Vases and candles in the pantry." The housekeeper hurried to her oven to finish the cake.

Jessie stared at the high parlor ceiling, wishing she could decorate the hanging candelabra with its long, curved arms. Then she had an idea. "Brilliant!" she chuckled and rushed to the pantry.

First she picked out a fancy bowl and some candles. Then she grabbed an apple from the fruit tray and sliced it. She dropped apple pieces into a plastic bag and added a handful of sunflower seeds. The bag was hidden in the bowl when she passed by the kitchen.

From the carton of decorations Jessie unwound a rope of golden tinsel. It followed her like an endless snake into the front hall. Jessie whistled softly. "Flummery, Captain Flummery," she called.

In a minute the black bird appeared at the top of the staircase. Jessie waved the garland. "Look, gold! It's treasure gold."

The mynah cocked his head. "Flummery's the name, treasure's my game?" He asked, puzzled. But he plopped down the steps, unable to resist the glittering tinsel.

"That's right, Captain Flummery. You're going to help me spread the treasure." Jessie tossed the end of the garland as high as she could toward the chandelier.

Flummery dove, catching the tinsel in his beak, then landed on the chandelier.

"Excellent!" Jessie grinned. She held up a slice of apple and began a slow circle under the chandelier. "Now, Captain, hang the treasure like this." She swooped her arm up and down. "Follow me and I'll give you this treat."

The bird hopped among the crystals, pulling the garland with his beak. "That's beautiful, Captain," Jessie smiled.

Flummery was so pleased with himself, he puffed his feathers and squawked proudly, "Treasure's my game." But whenever he squawked, he dropped the tinsel.

"Decorate first, talk later," Jessie commanded. "We are on a roll now, matey. Let's fix the parlor."

In no time the candelabra, the table, the windows and the fireplace were all swagged with shiny gold, red, and blue festoons. While the mynah chomped his reward, Jessie arranged a centerpiece of party hats and candles for the table. As a crowning touch, she stuck a hat on the mantel's carved lion head.

"We're not done yet, Captain, so don't fall asleep. Come on outside."

Jessie held a string of gold letters and showed Flummery where to drape it across the porch. Soon HAPPY BIRTHDAY sparkled from the roof. Perched on the flagpole, the bird jabbered "happy, happy."

Uncle MacKenzie's little car chugged along Wickham Lane and stopped beside the Cottage. Two tall men opened the doors and unfolded themselves from the auto.

"Look who I brought to the party," Uncle Mac shouted.

"Dad!" Jessie cried.

"Jessie!" he answered, swinging her around with a dizzy hug. "We've all missed you!"

Everyone talked at once while Brother Nile and Brother MacKenzie admired the decorations. Mrs. Merryweather welcomed them in her best apron.

They were about to go inside when Mr. Wong's delivery van arrived. Tommy jumped out with Trouble clinging to his shoulder. "Pop sent two kinds of ice cream and fortune cookies for the party. Thanks for the ride, Pop."

"Thanks, Mr. Wong," they called after the van.

When Trouble spotted Wickham, he bounced to the ground. The two cats claimed opposite ends of the porch for a staring contest.

"They'll work out a compromise," Uncle MacKenzie laughed. "As soon as Trouble remembers who is the boss on Wickham Lane. Now let's have some punch. I'm thirsty."

Uncle Mac led them into the parlor. "Take a bow, Jessie, these are the finest decorations we've ever had for our celebration."

Jessie passed the paper hats while Tommy lit

the candles. Mrs. Merryweather brought a tray of sandwiches. Uncle MacKenzie ladled pink punch into glass cups. Each person was served a cup with a wedge of pineapple and a strawberry floating on top.

They all sat down to their feast.

"I propose a toast," Jessie's father said, lifting his punch. "To Great-Aunt Carpathia, many happy returns." They clinked their cups.

"Delicious," they all agreed. Everyone was ready for second helpings when Wickham strolled into the parlor, Trouble tagging behind.

"Where have you cats been?" Mrs. Merryweather asked. "I'll bet you smelled food."

Jessie whispered to Tommy, "Visiting old friends, you know where."

Tommy nodded. "Trouble was showing off his new collar. Come on, fella, get up on your chair. Good boy, here's your sandwich." The big orange cat stood on his hind legs with his forepaws on the table. In a few bites he gobbled down an entire turkey sandwich.

"That is one monster feline," Brother Nile shook his head. "Watch out, he's eating his party hat!"

"Not the hat, not the hat!" Tommy plunked his cat on the floor. Trouble looked as if he were used to being told to stop eating things.

"Look, Wickham, I made a sardine sandwich,

especially for you." Jessie placed a plate on the table and patted a chair. But Wickham, utterly disgusted, refused to eat like humans. Jessie set his plate on the hearth.

"Flummery deserves a treat, too. He helped me decorate."

Jessie poured punch into a saucer; then added pineapple and strawberry pieces. After one sharp whistle, the mynah cruised the staircase and landed on the mantel. He ripped the fruit to shreds and slurped his punch.

While they were finishing their sandwiches, they heard a bell clanging on the front porch. "Must be the postman," Uncle MacKenzie said, rising to answer the door. He returned carrying a small square package.

This is addressed to you, Jessie."

"It's from, it says, Carpathia Wickham of Wickham Manor. How could that be?"

"Maybe she decided to send a present instead of receiving one," her father suggested. "Open it and find out."

Tommy leaned over the box. "Could I have these stamps for my collection? They're really old."

"Sure, but look at this weird postmark," Jessie whispered. "That date can't be true. It's too long ago."

When she unwrapped the paper, Tommy

quickly folded it and hid it in his pocket. "I'll check this out later," he told her.

Jessie lifted a transparent globe from the box. She carefully placed the globe on its stand for everyone to see. Inside the glass three tiny figures in old-fashioned dresses held hands in a circle.

"It's a musical toy," Mrs. Merryweather guessed. "Turn the key."

Jessie wound a little brass key. The three dolls whirled around to "London Bridge is Falling Down." When the verse ended they tilted backward, flipping their skirts over their faces and showing their pantaloons. They popped upright and danced again when the song started over.

Everyone burst out laughing at the silly dance. "What unusual behavior for proper young ladies," the housekeeper giggled.

"Cousin Cristobal and Cousin Willie," Jessie said.

"Who?" Tommy wanted to know.

"Girls in a story book I found upstairs—oh, never mind."

"Those South American cousins," the Gordon brothers nodded to each other.

"Who are you all talking about?" Tommy demanded, quite annoyed. "Anyway, the girl in the yellow dress looks kind of like you, Jess."

She punched his arm. "I wouldn't be caught in

public wearing a stupid dress with pantaloons!" Now she was annoyed.

"Ouch!" Tommy complained. "You should be called Rocky. That's the mountain you should be named for."

"Time for cake," Mrs. Merryweather shushed them. She cut slices of chocolate cake heaped with coconut frosting. "We have two flavors of ice cream. A scoop of both for everyone? I thought so."

Trouble begged a bite of cake, while Wickham lapped his spoonful of ice cream. Flummery had settled into a black lump above the fireplace, napping under his wings. He missed dessert.

"I almost forgot the fortune cookies," Tommy thumped his head. Mrs. Merryweather had arranged them in a silver dish. "Close your eyes and choose," Tommy said as he served the cookies.

"There's an extra one," Jessie noticed.

"It must be for Flummery," Tommy decided. The mention of fortune had awakened the mynah. Eagerly he pecked his cookie, destroying the strip of paper as well.

"Gold and pearls, pearls and gold!" Flummery strutted, vain as ever.

"I guess that's all we'll learn of the Captain's future," Uncle MacKenzie laughed as paper bits scattered to the hearth. "My fortune says, I will travel to distant lands seeking knowledge. Sounds like a trip for the science museum."

Mrs. Merryweather read, " 'Your next endeavor will bring success.' I must try that new recipe for gingerbread."

Tommy held up his hand. " 'You will find adventure in another world.' Does that mean I'll be an astronaut?"

" 'Something you love has been returned to you,' " Nile read. "That must be you, Jessie. Now it's your turn."

"My fortune says, 'You will find your Heart's Desire,' " Jessie recited. She had an idea.

"Dad, when you look at that picture, what do you see?" She pointed to the big gold frame. It was dark, completely blank.

"Why, just what it says," he answered. "It's Heart's Desire Cottage."

They all watched the picture as the misty glass gradually cleared. The cottage appeared, shining with fresh paint. The bushes had been trimmed.

"Perfect," the brothers agreed.

"We're in the painting, too!" Jessie cried.

One by one their images brightened. First, the brothers with their arms linked. Then Mrs. Merryweather at the pantry door. Jessie sat on the porch swing. Tommy leaned against the railing with Trouble sitting on his shoulder. Flummery perched on the flagpole.

"Here comes Wickham around the corner," Jessie said. "He's bringing the key."

"Look, there's someone in the tower," Tommy pointed.

"Great-Aunt Carpathia, I do believe," Uncle MacKenzie said.

"She always loved a good party," his brother smiled.

"I recognize that hat with the feathers," Mrs. Merryweather nodded.

"Happy Birthday, Aunt Carpathia," Jessie called. "Thank you for the present!" When the lady in the tower waved her lace handkerchief, they all waved back.

"Now I shall propose a toast." Uncle MacKenzie raised his punch cup. "Happy Birthday to us all."

"To us all," they chorused.

"Happy, happy," Flummery squawked. Trouble meowed in a rather small voice for such a large cat. Wickham added his low, rumbly meow.

"Here's to our Heart's Desire," Uncle MacKenzie beamed.

"Heart's Desire," they all said.